'An alternately inspiring and heartbreaking keyhole glimpse of a world the author believes disappeared with the advent of the bulldozers and the glossy blueprints for a miles better city'

Glasgow Evening Times

'It's hard not to be seduced by McGill's heartfelt mourning for something lost'

Time Out

'A very sure touch and gentle humour . . . Many of these stories deal with tenement children – the innocence of their cruelties, the oddities of their friendships. McGill captures their language and their plight, their exuberance and fancies'

Glasgow Herald

'McGill's interwoven short stories portray characters as vivid and bizarre as any found in the magical realism novels of South America . . . (he) has captured the Glasgow idiom and made a quite brilliant debut'

Edinburgh Evening News

'Like (Alasdair Gray), McGill succeeds in presenting a past from which nostalgia is largely expurgated . . . The episodes stand as separate stories welded into a novel by a progressive concern for the main characters and by a sense of the tenement having a life of its own which all these lives are a part'

Chapmans

John McGill was born in Glasgow in 1946 and went to school and university in that city. Following teacher-training, he taught in schools in the Orkney Islands, the Shetlands and Germany. Since 1980, he has lived in Lincoln with his wife, three daughters and a small, fat Labrador dog, and has taught in a small secondary school on the edge of the Lincolnshire Wolds. He has written short stories and poetry for many years in his brief moments of respite from teaching and has had several stories published in magazines and anthologies. *That Rubens Guy*, which has received widespread acclaim, is his first published collection. John McGill is now working on a novel.

THAT RUBENS GUY

Stories from a Glasgow Tenement

John McGill

CORGI BOOKS

THAT RUBENS GUY
A CORGI BOOK 0 552 13760 X

Originally published in Great Britain by
Mainstream Publishing Ltd

PRINTING HISTORY
Mainstream edition published 1990
Corgi edition published 1991

This book is set in 10/12pt Plantin by
County Typesetters, Margate, Kent

Corgi Books are published by Transworld Publishers Ltd, 61–63 Uxbridge Road, Ealing, London W5 5SA, in Australia by Transworld Publishers (Australia) Pty Ltd, 15–23 Helles Avenue, Moorebank, NSW 2170, and in New Zealand by Transworld Publishers (N.Z.) Ltd, Cnr Moselle and Waipareira Avenues, Henderson, Auckland.

Made and printed in Great Britain by
BPCC Hazell Books
Aylesbury, Bucks., England
Member of BPCC Ltd

To Matty and Alex

THE TENEMENT LAY-OUT

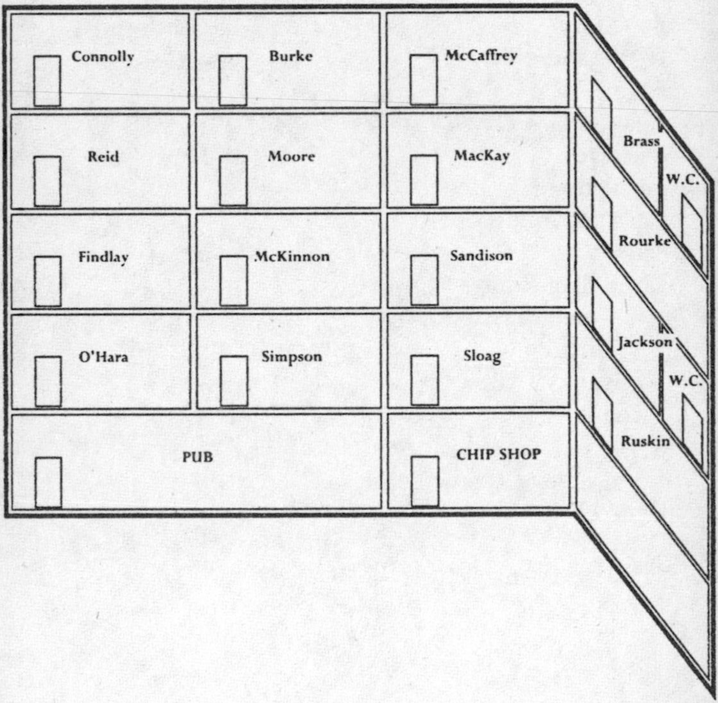

Connolly
Burke
McCaffrey
Brass
Reid
Moore
MacKay
W.C.
Findlay
McKinnon
Sandison
Rourke
O'Hara
Simpson
Sloag
Jackson
W.C.
PUB
CHIP SHOP
Ruskin

Contents

On a Saturday Morning in April 9
Freddy 27
Zoo Story 29
Wullie and Billy 43
Elsie 54
Thomas D. Forsyth 64
Pleasure 67
My Tony 85
Love and Mongooses 95
Angels 102
The Fall of Bumpstead Ruskin 112
The Three Brass Budgies 125
Tiger 148
The Stinky Ocean 152
Baroque 162
Blush 170
Granny Sloag's Secret 185
Limpy Dan 194
Cowgirl 199
The Sweary-man's Gold 219

On a Saturday Morning in April

Auld McKinnon lived under a mosquito net in a tent in the second house, second landing, and Keeking Thomas lived with the powerful cross-eyed tribe of Reids in the first house, third landing, and together they protected all four landings, all sixteen families in the close.

Keeking Thomas was eight and had been actively keeking for three years, during which Auld McKinnon had seen off the multitudinous lurkers and snappers without recourse to the elephant gun. Such were the comings and goings between houses that locked doors would have been a mere nuisance for most of the families, and Keeking Thomas went relatively unhindered on his Saturday morning tours. He keeked in their doors, beginning at Big Jessie's fourth door, fourth landing and finishing at Big Elsie's first door, first landing. On his way back to his own house he would stop outside Auld McKinnon's open door, where there were two railings missing and he could hang with his legs hooked across the bannister and his upside-down cross-eyes looking through the door to the misty mosquito net and catalogue his keekings.

On a morning in April, a memorable Saturday and the last of their joint protectorate, his catalogue ran thus:

> . . . seen The Man With The Painted Heid riding Mrs Brass she's a right hoor he shouts oof oof oof and the paint's just polish really it runs doon his neck – swing swing swingity swing – seen Mrs Simpson peeing in the

basin in the middle of the flerr, Margaret Moore puts her legs up on the chair and pulls her nylons up – seen Mr Sandison sleeping on the couch with pound notes in his ears and Mr Findlay seen me and I ran like shit he says I catch you you wee bugger I catch you at that again I'll mollicate you I'll murder you you wee skelly-eyed effer just mind your ain effing business. Bastit, I'm no as skelly as my mammy or my big sister or my wee sister Eileen she's the worst a mile, one eye looks to Paisley the other looks to Charing Cross – swing swing swingity swing – that John Findlay's a stuckup bastit he's spoiled rotten his da never hits him Wullie McCann could knock fuck oot of him any day no bother at all. Never seen Pat MacKay he gets steaming on one pint he goes in at twenty past nine and comes oot at hauf past singing 'Follow Celtic' and he staggers up the stair you never get any money aff him Mr Sandison's the best he gies you two-bob bits when he's steaming and once he gied Dom Moore a ten-bob note he was that drunk he spends hunners and hunners and he shags lots of women in places – swing swing swingity swing – I wait ootside the pub and sometimes Mr Burke losses his legs and his banjo and you take them up the stair for him and you get money – John Rourke's left the school he's on the broo I really like him you get money aff him. Seen my mammy she's got a big fight this morning she's fighting that Lily Simpson she's dancing with the radiogram that song again that Bing Crosby she gets dizzy – that Lily Simpson's a right hoor my mammy'll murder her smart as a brush no messing – swing swing – I can see right doon to the close I can see Sparky he's on the bottom step he bit me one time – swing swing swing swingity swing – he's a pure wee bastit . . .

*

Saturday milk a pint in each hand, young Jessica stopped a yard before the bottom step where Sparky the potlicker lay growling through a dream of rats. Sparky rose to his full five inches and snarled. Jessica snarled back. She was scared of Sparky but twice as scared of what Big Jessie, her mother, might do if the milk were lost.

'Away you dug. Get away or I'll murder you.'

Her kick was too tentative – a mere offering of soft flesh to willing snappers.

'Oh Mammydaddymammydaddymammydaddymammy-daddy Mammy Daddy.'

She danced roared screamed and clung hard to the milk bottles while Sparky dangled and swung from the fat above her left knee. The scream echoed up the spiral well of the staircase to the second landing where Keeking Thomas swung, and to the fourth, to the house opposite the lavatory where Big Jessie leg-locked The Man With The Painted Heid and drummed her heels on his thin white bum.

'Stop that a minute, will you,' she said, beginning to unwind her legs.

'Oof, oof, oof,' he said.

'Stop it, I said. That's that Jessica, I'll kill her so I will.'

'Oof.'

'Will you STOP it! I'll kill that Jessica.'

Secretly relieved, The Man With The Painted Heid rolled aside and lay back, panting. He had bronchitis.

Big Jessie pulled her skirt down and went out barefoot and sparely covered to the landing.

'That you Jessica? Jessica, is that you, hen? Je-e-essica!'

Jessica, shaken free, was running upstairs still clutching the Saturday milk and still aroar with rage and shock. She spurned the ministrations of big motherly Elsie O'Hara on the first landing, of Auld McKinnon on the second and of the busybodies ranged left and right on the third. At the top she did not fall howling into her mother's arms but delivered up the Saturday milk and turned downstairs again to the close. The savaged knee poured blood into her boot and her eyes were tear-blinded, but the step was sure. She wheeled left at the bottom into the backcourt where the middens were. Sparky was absorbedly rummaging in his favourite bin, happy and oblivious to the threat. She gripped him hard, one hand on the throat, the other on the left hind leg.

'Bastit dug,' she said.

She carried him back into the close. She had her gallery now, her Saturday gatherers on stairs and landings, and she played to it. She lifted Sparky ceremoniously to head-height and displayed him.

'Bastit dug.'

Elsie O'Hara saw what was coming and screamed. Big Jessie was fighting her way downstairs, pushing through the crowd. The stairwell held its breath, and Sparky, tuning in to the fear, began to whine.

'R-r-r-r-r-r-r-r-r-r-r-r-r-r-a-a-a-a-a-a-a-a-a-a-a-a-a!'

Jessica bit into the leg, the left hind leg, high up in the wide part. The whine became a squeal as she passed through fur to flesh. Sparky writhed, convulsed, squealed his hurt astonishment to the skylight, but her grip was as sure now as it had been earlier on the milk bottles, and he remained captive and tortured until Big Jessie arrived and took Jessica lightly by the hair.

Jessica set the potlicker carefully down.

'Deserved you right,' she said, reasoning with him. Tooth for tooth, leg for leg – she was content with that, her fury was spent, the affair was ended.

'Come on up and get your cornflakes, hen,' Big Jessie said. 'That dug wants destroying, so it does, it's a bloody nuisance, I'll tell the polis on it, so I will.'

The neighbours clucked their agreement and parted ranks to let them upstairs.

Auld McKinnon, relieved that danger had again been seen off without gunfire, reset the safety-catch of the elephant gun, and felt, through his relief, a grim conviction that each crisis cost him a little more than the one before. Back in his tent, he hung the elephant gun on its post by the bunk, stooped under the mosquito net and lay on his bunk, eyes closed, writing his logbook and pondering.

Thirty years under canvas and under this same mosquito net had suffered him not a single hour of unbroken sleep. The task allowed only snatched minutes, mere quarter-hours of eased vigilance; and it was often during such intervals that danger saw its chance and leapt, as now. Jessica from the top landing – a brave strong child but a child too often alone, too often at the mercy of the lurkers and snappers – he worried for, as he worried for all of them. Without the services of the boy, the Keeker, it would have become impossible over the last few years.

On every landing there were child-wide gaps in the bannister; the second-storey lavatory was about to collapse into the backcourt; there was not a whole gasmantle anywhere in the building, nor a whole pane in the skylight; at night the rats took over, too many even for the battalions of cats and the potlicker-packs; but there was no way the landlord could be induced or compelled to spend on a property already long condemned. It might be years, notwithstanding the demolition order, and Auld McKinnon did not feel overburdened with years.

This newest crisis, this third-landing show-down between the scorpion and the dancing she-ape, this bloody Saturday sideshow which had set the women clucking and the men betting and the children romancing for a day now, was symptomatic. As he aged, as his eyes and ears dulled, so manners changed, and dangers assumed forms beyond his apprehension.

The years of the bombs had been an interval of cohesion, when the shared threat had exposed the pettiness of traditional hatreds – when, if he remembered rightly, Jock Simpson, father of the same scorpion, Lily, led the team whose duty it was to transport the giantess, Aggie Reid – she who collapsed in a dead faint at the first hint of the siren – to the shelter.

The danger now, it seemed, came all from the inside.

That Lily Simpson. She had returned to the tenement, to her dead grandmother's house, with a dull, brutish man called McCaffrey and two monstrous screeching children; returned to inherit her mother's position as fighter and biter and scratcher, as troublemaker-in-chief, and to bring to it a new, dry nastiness. Where Jane Simpson had bitten and clawed to protect her brood from real and imagined menace and had nurtured the tigerish in them out of some sense of the right thing, Lily, her eldest, placed the fighting first, and used her children as a pretext, a means of legitimizing her tyrannous authority over many of the other women. Invincibly stupid in most things, she brought delicate skill to the art of terror, so that no showdown found her without a safe psychological advantage over her opponent. In the year since her return she had effectively cowed most of the women of the upper landings, and a few further afield.

Within that upper domain, since Big Jessie had given herself shamelessly and totally to The Man With The Painted Heid, her chief rival was Aggie Reid, mother of Keeking Thomas and five others, who shared in equal measure her own wildly skewed eyes and the tightly curled black hair of their father, Tom Reid, who worked shifts and played out his days, like Wullie Moore next door, as a dim presence, a creaking irritation behind the bed-curtains, calling out for tea and quiet and chamberpots.

A bad business. Auld McKinnon opened his eyes long enough to check that the elephant gun hung correctly angled on its post. Then worry, for so long the spoiler of his rest, had done his nerves in till they could face it no more, and he slept.

The tenement, stirred by Jessica's encounter with Sparky, was warming to its Saturday rituals and gearing itself for the big fight. Lily's opening had come on the Thursday, the day when each household had received a brown envelope containing intimation of the coming demolition, and a form on which the tenants were invited to consider the rehousing options and to indicate their preferences in rank order, one, two and three. Lily, as dominant in stairhead gossip as in every other sphere, told a dozen assorted and overlapping groups about her witty first preference:

'Anywhere as long as it is a hundred mile away from that bitch Reid,' she told them in her best posh-precise English, just as she had written it. Then she went on with her feared and ferocious hyena-howl, which bullied all but the bravest into nods and lickspittle laughter.

'A hundred mile,' she would repeat, closing her eyes and pressing the back of her clenched fist to her forehead in a gesture of paralytic mirth, 'from that BITCH Reid.'

When this *bon mot* reached Aggie Reid, as it had to, her response was characteristically simple. She spread it abroad that *her* first choice had been, 'Anywhere as long as it's a thousand mile away fae that hoor Lily Simpson and her daft man, they should be in the loonybin anyway.'

The women laughed with her willingly enough, but nervously, wary lest Lily or any of her spies should be lurking. And Aggie Reid, too, would press her message home: 'In the loonybin, that's what I wrote, ask Reid, he seen me writing it, so he did.'

So it was that on the Friday morning, while Aggie Reid waltzed to Bing Crosby, while she Dorothy-Lamoured across the kitchen carpet in a half-swoon of moonlit romance, the letterbox clicked and a ripped-open Players packet floated to the lobby floor and settled against the coal-bunker. The pencil scrawl, faint and almost lost among the creases, read:

> You have called me a hoor so I will fight you on Saturday at 12. Meet me on the 3ird story, it is you whoos a hoor more liker it.
>
> Yours truly
> Mrs Lily McCaffrey

Neither acceptance nor refusal was solicited, and no reply was expected. Lily would be on the third landing at the appointed time, sharpening her nails; the audience would have draped itself on the stairs and bannisters; and Aggie Reid, rolling up her sleeves, would step out to meet her.

Tony Sandison was roused from fitful sleep by a low businesslike tap on the door. He sat up on the sofa, cascading fivers, and placed himself: Saturday morning, a big Friday, a big Thursday, four winners at Newmarket, Fat Elsie, Skinny Lucy, sherry, brandy, Fat Elsie again, home at three to bristling emptiness, three kicks splitting the new white hardboard of the door, dreams.

'Come on in. It's open. I'll just lift the blinds.'

Barney the Book stepped into the murk.

'Hi Tone.'

Tony raised the blind on the big window. Fivers spilled

on to the white sofa, the white Axminster. He rubbed his eyes.

'Hi Barney. How's it gaun?'

'Mina away tae her mother's again, eh? Many times you broke that door noo? Can you no get yoursel a key, for Christ's sake?'

'She'll be back. What can I do for you, Barney?'

Barney thrust his hands deep into his trenchcoat pockets, bowed his head, and began to draw shapes in the pile of the carpet with his toe.

'It's a blue do, Tony my son, a blue do. Big Elkie's blazing.'

'Whit fur?'

It was not a real question, Tony knowing well enough the cause of Big Elkie's wrath, but an appeal for clemency. Barney understood, and was willing as ever to extend it, but it was part of the game, part of his gangster rôle, that he should stay quiet for a minute or two, staring at the floor, while Tony suffered.

'Christ Almighty, Barney, surely a wee fight on the stair doesnae coont?'

Barney wrote the numbers from one to nine, then switched to his left foot and wrote them again in descending order.

Tony pouted his lower lip and blew his innocence through it. 'I mean to say, Barney, Christ.'

'Everything coonts, Tony son. You know that. All bets up 30, 22 as used to be, 14 and 6 – they're Big Elkie's. Many you lifted so far?'

'Nine, ten, I'm no sure.'

'What odds?'

'Eleven-to-seven on the wee yin, five-to-two the draw.'

'Judges?'

'To be arranged. Pat MacKay and a couple of boys fae ootside.'

Barney, thinking, drew a face in the carpet, paused over the mouth, then completed it as an upward-curling ear-to-ear smile.

'Mm. Tell them their bets are transferred to Big Elkie, through me. Usual arrangements, same odds. OK?'

There was no altercation. Tony Sandison, who loved many women and drank cognac and Black Label whisky and handled more fivers than the rest of the tenement put together, smiled the smile that time and again disarmed Mina, his long-suffering wife, the winning smile of the mischievous boy accepting just rebuke, scratched his head, twirled a fiver in his right ear, rolled his eyes, and, permitting himself a small flurry of saving bravado, said 'Fair enough, Barn . . . if that's the way you want it.'

Barney turned to go. 'Must cost you a fortune in doors,' he said.

The children rehearsed the fight openly, eagerly, while their mothers affected shock and their fathers, contempt.

And while the building buzzed, while even the bitten Jessica and the breathless Man With The Painted Heid and the chidden Tony forgot their sufferings in happy expectation, Auld McKinnon slept.

Keeking Thomas heard his snores and saw for the first time the elephant gun unguarded on its post. He knew the odds, knew too the fightgame clichés – that a good big 'un will beat a good little 'un but, overridingly, a pro will beat an amateur. And for Lily Simpson, fighting was a way of life.

The gun. It was no less fearful this thing, this wondrous equalizer of odds, now that it was there for the lifting. He still trembled at the sight of it, at the blue sheen of its metal and the red warmth of its wood; and still more he trembled at its hidden death-dealing history. He knew too well that his mother – she who ran from mice and whose terror of the sirens was one of the tenement legends – would never be induced to touch it; that it was for him, Thomas the Keeker, to ensure that the cat-claws would never draw blood from his mother's eyes. The picture of Lily Simpson, holed and screeching and kicking her legs in the air like a stranded bug, danced thrillingly in his head, and he began with fine-tuned stealth to creep towards the tent.

Fear of the thing itself and terror of waking the old man gave him strength; it was monstrously heavy though, and he marvelled that the frail old snorer could heft it with such style. He cradled it in his arms and tiptoed out to the landing. Safely there, he tried holding it for use, tucking the butt into his shoulder and sighting along the barrel, but it was too long and much too heavy. Timorously, he fingered the safety-catch, the trigger-guard, the trigger itself. He grew bolder, and found he could support the weapon and direct it accurately if he rested the barrel on the bannister rail. It was a question now of finding a vantage point, noting it, and hiding in the lavatory until the fight began. From the staircase between the first and second landings, he decided, he would not be seen by the crowd and could still command almost a quarter of the third. A tricky shot it would be, at a tight angle, but with care and luck he might succeed in blowing the head off.

At eleven o'clock Lily McCaffrey, née Simpson, started her training routines. For five minutes she struck poses in front of the full-length mirror in her wardrobe door. Then she made her face. She plucked her eyebrows and pencilled them so that they almost met above her nose, then curled them up slightly at the sides. She brushed back her thick gypsy-black hair and bound it in a tight knot behind her head – so tight the skin was stretched and the bare white temples blazed. She daubed her lips screaming scarlet and practised snarls, first with all her teeth in, then, with only the lower set. She touched up her scarlet nails, breathed on them, touched them up again, and made trial assaults on her reflection, pouncing from various heights and angles. Practising, she warmed to the task: it was a good Saturday morning, with the promise of even better to come.

'Hey Tommy,' she called to the bed-recess, 'you watching this fight or just lying there rotting aw day?'

Her husband sat up and pulled aside the curtain.

'Just coming,' he said. 'You look really great, honest tae God.'

'Just you watch me murdering that bitch. Ya-ee-ee-ee-ee!'

She leapt at him, snarling, arching her hands and thrusting her nails at his face. The sudden ferocity frightened him, as it always did.

'Jesus Christ, Lily, save it for the real thing, right? And mind, she's big, right?'

'Oh-ho, don't worry, son. She's no that big I cannae reach her big skelly eyes.'

Those same eyes, at half-past eleven, were still closed in Bali. Aggie Reid had seen young Aggie off to her work at the tobacco factory, had packed the young children off to play, had emptied the chamberpots, had given Reid his mug of tea and his ham-and-tongue paste sandwich, and was not ready to let anyone or anything disturb her Saturday morning dance. Not till the clock on the mantelpiece chimed quarter-to did she lift the needle from the record and begin her warm-up. She worked in silence – Reid had his rights too, as a nightshift man, and sounds other than Bing Crosby would have disturbed his rest.

'Fucking bitch,' she said in her head, grabbing the invisible scrawny shoulders and shaking hard. 'Fucking animal. Fucking Protestant.' She pushed Lily to her knees, then, keeping a grip on the right shoulder with her left hand, she slapped her rival three times, hard on the side of the head with her right. She thought about a final kick, decided against it, and turned back to her own door, confining her remarks to an echo of what Jessica had said earlier to the vanquished Sparky:

'Deserved you right, so it did.'

She played the scene again, this time dragging the battered Lily by the hair to the bottom of the flight that led up to the fourth landing saying: 'Noo get back to your ain landing and stay there or I'll kill you the next time, so I will.'

This, allowing as it did the triumphal walk back along the third landing to her own door, pleased her.

'Back to your ain landing,' she repeated aloud.

The sound woke Reid, who called out from behind the curtain, 'Whit's that? That you, Aggie?'

'It's aw right Reid, I'm just going oot for a minute. I'll no be long,' she said.

Pat MacKay, third door, third landing, held his head under the tap for three minutes. He could hear the rising murmur of the crowd and the fat, loud voice of Rosie, his wife, who had been out there ten minutes since, lending her huge weight to the cause of third-landing solidarity. For him, an officially appointed judge, a late impartial appearance was required.

He dried his head on the net curtain, combed his hair with a craftsman's loving attention to the parting, knotted his tie in a brutally symmetric Windsor, put on his good striped funeral-jacket, and at 11.58 stepped out on to the landing.

Almost all of the women and children and some of the men had gathered on the stairs and landing to watch the spectacle and join in the sideshows. The hugged and pampered Jessica showed her wound; Old Granny Sloag called for the hanging of Bumpstead Ruskin who had yet again upended her in the space between his and her doors on the first landing; Tam Burke played requests on his banjo.

Tony's announcement of the transfer of bets and the judges' names – Pat MacKay and two outsiders from neighbouring blocks – brought no protests, but set long-practised arguments going among the older spectators about Lily's fight record and formulaic laments for the decline in moral standards that her reign betokened, as against her mother's. Jane Simpson, listening, kept modestly and loyally silent.

The Man From The Corporation, dispatched to check that everybody had received a rehousing form, arrived to find only empty houses and angry ungrateful husbands on the first two landings, and daunted by the festive multitude on the third, retreated back to the close and the welcoming sunny Road. On his way he passed Keeking Thomas on the first flight. Thomas did not notice him. He was taking up his stance with the elephant gun.

Great gun. marvellous. Fucking heavy, but. You hit elephants right between the eyes wi it seen it in the pictures that Jungle Jim wham, right there, kills them wi one bullet, bang, lovely. He's sleeping, daft auld bastit, lies in that tent never talks never eats never goes oot nothing. My mammy's a right killer Rocky Marciano's no in it she'll kill that Lily Simpson nae bother send for the cleaners. You put the bullets in there right under that thing you stick them in you lift that thing it's too stiff for me you just aim it like this, Jungle Jim, bang bang, right between the eyes. There's the skylight, there's the landing, I'll get her dead easy fucking hoor right in the heid, my mammy'll murder her nae bother. Aim right there lie the gun right there, stoating – cannae miss.

Smashing. He rested the barrel of the elephant gun on the bannister and settled into his assassin's crouch, curling the first two fingers of his right hand round the stiff trigger. It was 11.59.

A momentary flicker of his eyelid was enough for Auld McKinnon: the safety of the gun on its post had always been the first concern of his awakenings. He sat up and stretched himself awake and heard the shouts that signalled the entry of the combatants. His gravest fear – the moment of eased watchfulness, the unlatching of the gate that kept out the lurkers and snappers – had been realized. He reached the bannister and looked down at the tense crouching Keeker sighting the gun upwards at the third landing where Lily Simpson had begun her preparatory strut.

Never one for shouting – he had, in truth, uttered nothing aloud before a listener in some five or six years – Auld McKinnon tried to attract the boy's attention by waving his arms; that failing to break the marksman's concentration, he rattled the bannister and fell into an urgent groan like that of a dumb man desperate to deliver a message; finally, panic and despair broke the silence of years. He opened his mouth wide, strained for a syllable, and shouted.

It happened that his shout, loud in the moment of decision, concurred with the instant of silence, the communal bating of breath, which marked the start of the fight. The fragile stillness of the stairwell was shattered, and before the echo had died the crowd had abandoned the contest in a rush for the bannisters. Keeking Thomas did not have time to straighten up before Auld McKinnon reached him and stretched across his shoulders to grab the gun. He resisted, and finding the old man stronger, gave a despairing squeeze to the trigger. Nothing happened, of course – the ancient inner mechanism was long since incapable of movement – but the dreadful sight of the trigger being depressed spurred Auld McKinnon to a final urgent jerk that won the gun and sent the Keeker, in equal and opposite reaction, crashing against the railings. The metal, rotten in itself and based on rotten concrete, gave way, and he passed under the bannister, taking two of the bars with him.

He landed on his belly lengthways astride the iron bar that spanned the gap between the first landing and the staircase. By the time the spectators had seen through the gloom and could take in what was happening, the scene that presented itself was of Auld McKinnon, fuddled, clutching the gun and staring helplessly at the boy, who rolled on the bar, clung like a sloth for a terrible three seconds, and dropped fifteen feet to the close.

For the second time that morning the solidarity of crisis cancelled differences. Aggie Reid's steely hatred melted into panic, and she fell into the arms of her seconds. Lily Simpson rushed to her aid, and helped carry her into the Reid's house. The others began to tumble downstairs. Jessica, clinging to her mother's blouse and hirpling, was torn between envy of, and sincere solicitation for, the Keeker. 'He'll be even worser nor me,' she told the folk on either side of her. 'He'll be even deid.'

Some of the children ran to the Kenny Street Police Station, while Tony Sandison, the only telephone-subscriber in the building, went into his house to ring for an ambulance.

The Keeker had fallen providentially feet-foremost and his condition, though serious enough, was not critical.

The elephant gun, torn from the grasp of the stunned old man, was righteously smashed against the stairs and walls. And while Thomas the Keeker, the listener and prober whom they had been abusing and cursing and threatening for three years now, was borne whimpering on a stretcher to the ambulance, the communal rage was turned on the bent, silent old man, who was being asked by PC McGlaughlin to accompany him to the station. Lily Simpson finished ministering to the stricken mother in time to launch the most vehement attack:

'That is a fucking auld loony, that is. I've told them repeatedly that auld loony should be locked up and fling the key in the canal. I've told them repeatedly – they want tae hing him, so they dae.'

Her sentiments drew general endorsement; everyone, it seemed, had been demanding Auld McKinnon's permanent locking-away for years.

The prisoner did not respond to their abuse, or to PC McGlaughlin's gentler overtures. He stood clinging to the elephant gun that was not there any more, was nothing but a scattering of wood and metal on the stairs. No-one offered to get his shoes or his coat from the house on the second landing; it was a warm spring morning and he was dressed as always, apart from the faded carpet-slippers, for the outdoors. In answer not to the policeman's voice or to the mockery of the crowd, but to the gentle pressure on his arm, he let himself be led down to the close and out into the road, into the blinding sunlight.

A Saturday morning to remember – to pass on, magnified, to children and grandchildren. The wicked – Sparky the potlicker and Auld McKinnon the lunatic – had got their deserts; the virtuous – Jessica the dogbiter and Thomas the masterspy – were holy with wounds and bathed in love.

Nobody was in a hurry to return home while so much remained to be discussed, and Tony Sandison took advantage of this to silence them and, puffed with the vested authority of Big Elkie and Barney the Book, make his formal announcement:

'Ladies and gentlemen, all bets are declared null and void, stakes to be returned. All bets null and void.'

Freddy

I spit in their fat every night without fail – wheech – bang – swoosh! – right in the fucking middle. Lying swines, they say I pee in it as well, but I don't, Rita would murder me if she caught me at that, she would fling me in the fryer, no hesitation, and anyway, when I tried it once I was too scared and the pee wouldn't come. But it's bloody marvellous at night when the fryer's going its dinger and Rita's not looking – wheech bang – swoosh! – big juicies, right in the middle.

They think I'm a Tally and I'm over seventy, silly buggers. They think Freddy's short for Alfredo – that's a laugh, it's Alfredo that's long for Freddy, if they only but knew. Freddy Duff, Springfield Road; Dalmarnock born and bred; nearest I've been to sunny Italy's the pictures – that Sophia Loren, wow wow! Right enough, I speaka di Italiano when it suits me – just to kid the bastits.

I'm fifty-six, same age as Rita, but she won't look at me.

Tally women are the best in the world for rumpy-pumpy, no doubt about it. Rita, she's fifty-six, and she's killed two men – heart-attacks – wow! what a way to go.

Rita, Rita, Rita.

They hated us in the war, us Tallies. Bricks through the window, shit in the letter-box, abuse. We even got a petrol-bomb – that daft swine McGrogan blew three of his own stupid fingers off, no kidding.

Oh, Rita.

I take their water, that's the main reason they hate me. Seven every morning when the men are getting up for work I switch on the four taps and watch the water pouring out; then half-eight when the kids are getting ready for school I do it again. I keep the door locked and they go mad. Sometimes there's a queue of kids a mile long outside banging on that door. 'Mrs Lusardi, Mrs Lusardi, my mammy says can you tell Freddy tae stop running the watter, ma da needs a wash for his work!'

'Fuck your da,' says I to myself. Then I shout through the locked door, 'Ha! Your da he havva to wait! You wanta da chips, you no wanta da fucking things? I gotta washa da fucking spuds!'

Spuds my arse. I go into the back kitchen, and I sit in my chair, and I think about Rita, bare naked, creeping into my bed, and I watch and watch and watch the water pouring away. I've got four taps and they've only got one each and I'm at the bottom so they don't stand a chance, they get eff-all, not a bloody drop, ha, ha.

That's what I do – sit and watch the water and think about Rita, and then I think about all the silly bastids hitting their taps and fuming and cursing me blue in the face all the way up to the fourth storey and I laugh, ha, ha, and I think life's pretty good.

Zoo Story

Phil Findlay, stout Phil who worked alternate Saturdays, was worried. Usually he spent his Saturday off till midday enthroned behind the drapes of the bed recess while Bella his wife and Netta his daughter served him with ready-stirred cups of tea and the *Weekend Mail*, and the *Daily Record*. But this morning was different, and Bella, fluttering ulcered Bella, was worried too. She had slept badly in the night and finally wakened a good hour later than usual, at nearly six o'clock. So now there were a bare two hours left, and the sideboard hadn't been polished and the windows were clattie. Netta had emptied the chamber-pots and was setting the fire while Bella wiped the mirrors and nagged and fretted and Phil shouted at them to get the kettle on for his shaving water and the shammies ready for the windows. John, nine and bitter, was lifting things – socks and shoes and rubber garters and shoepolish tins – from under things and mumbling his surly resentment at the usurpation of his Saturday morning.

'Think it was the Queen or somebody – instead of just another one of Alastair's tarts.'

'Shut up you,' said Netta. 'This one's a toff. Bad enough her coming here to this dump without we at least clean it up a bit for her.'

Alastair was nineteen, fond of himself, and good with girls. He was normally stringing two or three along at a time, but for a month now had been steady with Jacqueline, whose father was something big in the zoo and who came from a house with stairs and a bathroom and gardens front and back; and he was bringing her to meet the family. John, generally at a loss about his brother's pursuit of women, tentatively approved of this one because of the zoo connection – hence his small contribution to the preparations for the visit. Phil, who would never have lifted nor been expected to lift a hand in housework, was playing his part by rising – vacating his draped sanctuary some two hours early – and by shaving. He played it, to be sure, ungrudgingly, anxious to support his son in such a promising venture.

But he was worried; he was worried about many a thing, but most pressingly about the toilet. It was a fear that beset them whenever there was a visitation from another ambit – that at some point the question of a trip to the second-storey lavatory might arise. Part of their daily and nightly ritual though it was, they could well imagine the effect of that cavernous hole, that measureless emptiness, that welter of rotten planks and peeling plaster and cat's pee and coal and rats and vomit, on effête, unaccustomed nerves.

Upright now in his long drawers, he gave voice to their shared dread.

'Hope to Christ she'll no want the closet,' he said, glancing up at the big brass key, his own handywork, that hung on a nail by the side of the door.

'She'll just have to put up with it,' said Netta, unwilling to concede too much to the other side. '*We* have to.'

They came as arranged at half-ten. They negotiated the door from the landing without untowardness, but got awkwardly squeezed together in the inner doorway because Alastair had been uncertain of whether to come through first or to usher the girl in instead. In his hesitancy he tightened his grip on her arm, which became painfully twisted across her back and caused her smile of greeting to screw into a grimace. Already it was clear that his association with this exotic creature had robbed Alastair of his customary savoir faire. His cheeks were red.

'Eh . . . Ma, Da . . . this is Jacqueline.'

'Pleased to meet you, hen.' Phil shook the timidly offered hand. 'Come on in and sit down.'

'Hello,' said Netta, pointedly loud. 'I'm his only favourite sister.'

Jacqueline smiled, princesslike. She wore a tailored suit, peacock blue, with a skirt that reached fashionably to her kneecaps and added to her already daunting problems that of deciding whether to let it ride above the knees when she sat down, or pull it over them. She opted, with demure unsuccess, for the latter course.

Bella poured tea. There were cups and saucers for all except Phil, whose anxiety to please could never have carried him to the length of abandoning his blue-striped pint-and-a-half mug. On the table – for John another bonus and consolation – was a plate heaped with fancy things: French cakes and fern cakes and slices of Swiss roll.

Bella fluttered. 'There's sugar and milk, hen, just help yourself.'

'Thanks very much, Mrs Findlay. I'll take a wee spot of milk – I don't take sugar in tea, but I always take it in coffee. Funny that, isn't it?'

John, sitting on the low stool by the fireside, stared and listened, and his fascination with her pale thin face, her neatly trimmed and shaped red-blonde hair, her queenly clothes, her long elegant legs, her soundless delicate sipping of her tea and her sugared accent, cancelled all his resentment. He ached to address her, to get the full story of the zoo, but knew he would blush if he tried to open his mouth.

'I cannae drink that coffee,' said Bella. 'It gies me a rotten taste in my mouth, so it does. Isn't that right, Phil?'

'Aye.'

'I drunk it waance and it gied me a right rotten taste. That was afore the war, wasn't it Phil?'

'Aye, that was years ago.'

'Aye, it was afore the war. I just cannae look at the stuff – even the smell turns my stomach – I like that cocoa, but. I like that for a wee change sometimes.'

'Yes, cocoa's really nice,' said Jacqueline. 'I sometimes take it at bedtime, just to settle me.' Her teeth looked as if they had been chiselled and filed and polished to a perfect filmstar symmetry, and her voice was like faintly sour milk. She sounded, John thought, like people on the wireless.

Phil pointed to the heaped plate. 'Have a cake, hen, you look like you could do with a bit of fattening up – doesn't she, Bella?'

'Oh, Phil, you're terrible, so you are. She's just a lovely shape, nice and slim. That suits you, that costume. Blue's nice.'

'Thank you.' Jacqueline lifted a piece of Swiss roll and balanced it on her saucer. 'I shouldn't really eat cakes, it's terrible.'

'Christ, wait till you're like me, then you can start worrying, heh?' Phil lifted his arms a little to display his body in its full grossness. 'Fourteen stone in my stocking-feet, there you are.'

Netta interrupted. 'Shut up, you. We're no wanting to hear about your belly.' In the presence of this ethereal stranger, she was painfully conscious of her own spreading middle. Phil smacked his toothless gums together in mock rage, performing for the visitor.

'See the way they talk to their faither – scandalous, isn't it?'

Jacqueline smiled and sipped her tea.

There was a silence for a while, relieved only by the

prim clink of cup on saucer and Phil's slurping and lip-smacking. John, desperate for the zoo story but too nervous to trust his voice, looked as pushingly as he could at his father and his brother, willing them to speak; but Phil's mouth was invincibly full of cake and Alastair had decided his tie-pin needed adjusting and Bella was fussing with the tea-cosy, so it was Netta who finally delivered him from the rack.

'Smashing morning, isn't it?'

'Oh yes,' said Jacqueline, becoming still milkier in her relief at being offered a topic she could enlarge upon. 'It's really lovely. I was just saying to Alastair on the way in – this is maybe the only summer we'll get.'

'I know, it's terrible, so it is.' Bella, not trusting herself to sit down without misadventure, and feeling her ulcer beginning to act up, was checking that the gas was switched off.

'Aye, it's terrible.' Phil was still mauling a French cake in his gums.

'I know, it's terrible,' said Netta.

The silence was reasserted. Perched on the edge of the stool, John eased himself forward and surveyed the guest, whose smooth glued-together knees were level with his eyes.

Filmstar legs – immaculately slim, in pale shiny stockings. The shoes were blue, to match the skirt and jacket, and he wondered where on earth she could find polish for them. The face was small-featured, angelically pale, with a fine tracery of veins coming through the powder at the temples. The mouth, carefully and delicately lipsticked, was an exquisite little scratch of vermilion, eye-catchingly beautiful against the marble-whiteness of the surrounding skin.

'Aye,' somebody said.

'So yous two for the dancing the night?' Netta asked.

'Suppose so,' said Alastair. 'Up the Land, or maybe the Locarno.'

'Oh aye, go to the Locarno, son. That Barrowland's no a nice place.' In Bella's generally fearful vision of the universe, Barrowland, the local dance hall, figured as the purest of horrors, a hive of razor-slashers, knifers, bicycle-chainers, brass-knucklers.

'Och Ma, Barrowland's a lot cheaper – and anyway, it's nothing like what you think.' Alastair had had this same discussion with his mother on most of the previous ninety Saturdays.

'Still and all, I worry myself sick when you go there.'

Jacqueline came to her aid. 'I know what you mean, Mrs Findlay. My mother's just the same about Barrowland. It's got a really bad reputation.'

'See!' said Bella, enjoying a rare moment of triumph, and talking mostly to Phil, who had ridiculed her often enough for her over-anxiety, and who now decided a change of theme was called for.

'So your old man's in the zoo, eh? What is he – waan of they chimpanzees?'

Bella and Netta scowled their disapproval, but Jacqueline laughed.

'Well no – actually he's an assistant supervisor. He worked as a keeper for twelve years. He's in charge of all the reptiles now.'

'Oh.' Bella shuddered. 'I hate animals, don't I, Phil? They rats, I'm awful feart of them.'

This was too much for John. 'It's no rats, Ma. It's reptiles – snakes and lizards and that.'

'Oh I hate they snakes as well, don' I, Phil? I hate them even worse.'

'Aye,' said Phil.

'I really really hate them – even pictures of them. I don't know how anybody could . . . I think they should all be done away with, don't I, Phil?'

'Aye,' said Phil.

'Then her da wouldnae have a job, would he?' said Netta, challenging.

'Yes, that's true,' said Jacqueline. 'He really loves snakes. They're quite interesting really, once you get to know them.'

'Aye, her da's been everywhere, so he has. He's been all over the world, nae kidding,' said Alastair. 'He's been to that Africa, even. Hasn't he?'

'Oh yes,' said Jacqueline, 'and he's been to America quite a few times.'

Phil absent-mindedly held out his mug for Bella to stir his tea. He was interested now. 'That right? That's smashing. How did he like that America?'

'Very nice. He went to Florida.'

They talked with freedom now, and John, who had nine animal books and a scrapbook of photographs cut from newspapers and magazines, probed the visitor with questions about her father's travels and the eating habits of alligators, while Bella shuddered and took each fresh revelation as further proof of her view that life was a darkened labyrinth with blood-lusting predators lurking behind every corner and where the only safe course was to do nothing, say nothing, go nowhere.

The teapot and the cake-plate were empty, and the young lovers were about to leave. They were planning to go into town for some shopping in the afternoon – probably for a ring, Netta informed John in a whisper – and to Jacqueline's parents for tea.

The communal sense of accomplishment and relief was destroyed, however, when Jacqueline, standing up and straightening her skirt, said: 'I wonder if I could just visit your toilet before I go, Mrs Findlay?'

The Findlays looked at each other, then at the key. Phil

rolled his eyes and shrugged resignedly.

'The key's up there, hen. The lavvy's at the end of the landing – Netta'll show you.'

Netta reached up to take the key from its nail.

'Follow me,' she said brightly. They went out into the landing. After a minute, Netta came back.

'Thank you very much, Netta,' she said, imitating Jacqueline's silky tone.

'Shut up, you. You shouldnae make a fool of the lassie. She's awful nice,' said her mother.

'Aye, she's a nice lassie,' Phil agreed. 'Nice and plain.'

'Hope she's aw right in that place,' said Netta, anxious to show that her impersonation had expressed curiosity and not mere resentment.

'I hope so,' said Phil.

The place was thick with ghosts. A high-vaulted cavern, bigger than three of their living-rooms combined, square, with the toilet-bowl diagonally opposite the door, it served the eight families of the first and second landings. In past times it had functioned as a storage area, and the wrecked cupboards and shelves still clung to the walls. Left of the door the Jacksons still kept their coal-bunker. From the bowl you could look down through the spaces in the floorboards to the backcourt thirty feet below. There was no light. Some people used the place at night, venturing forth with a candle or an electric torch, but most preferred chamberpots in the warmth of the house. On winter evenings it was the main play-area for the children, and their games were all ghosts and werewolves and murder and The Man With The White Sandshoes. There had been at least one real death there, when old man Jackson had collapsed with a heart attack and smashed his head on the bowl; and there were countless mythic deaths and madnesses that the children re-enacted in their play. In one corner was a full-length cupboard which still kept most of its door and was the putative den of The Man With The White Sandshoes, who was small and sly and silent and ate children and who lived real and terrifying in their hearts and in their chants and games.

Jacqueline turned the big brass key to lock herself in and instantly regretted it. Even now, on a bright April morning, the place was gloomy. The only light was from a small grating high above the bowl, and from the spaces in the floorboards in the same corner. From the door, the bowl seemed hideously distant, the space to be covered horribly chill and dark. Yet cover it she had to. Her need had been pressing enough at the start, in her nervousness at meeting the family for the first time: now, an hour and three cups of tea later, it was urgent. She let her eyes settle themselves to the murk, and leaving the key in the door, began to make her way towards the bowl. Her heels caught frighteningly in the floorboards a few times, and a scurrying in dim corners brought images of rats.

The bowl, safely reached, was a ghastly sight. The wooden seat had long since gone, and there remained a brutal perch, a cracked and pitted porcelain monster that stared up at her through the sick blue light. The urgency of her need prevailed over her fear, and she resolved to see the thing through, avoiding, if she could, any contact with the bowl. She pulled up her skirt, and was scared by the whiteness of her thighs in the gloom. Unnerved by her nakedness, she stood for some time with the skirt hitched stupidly to her waist, staring down at her own soft whiteness, at the monstrous cracked filth of the bowl, at the strips of daylight and the grey rooftops of the backcourt middens under her feet.

The myriad noises of the Saturday tenement funnelled into the shell-like void: the girning babies and the nagging wives and the carping or snoring men and the lovemakers and the eaters and drinkers and rollicking children and raucous radios merged in a primordial sigh – a throbbing pulse that mingled with her own heartbeat, with the throb of blood in her own blue temples – and she swayed. She pulled her knickers to her knees, perched herself as high as she could on her toes to keep her legs clear of the bowl and began, tremulously, to lower her bottom to the hollow of it. Doing so, she looked towards the door and realized that from there, where she hung cold and bare and guardless above that awful hole, it was invisible.

After quarter of an hour they began to argue, the women sure that something was wrong, the men timidly ignorant of the habits of such a one as Jacqueline and insisting they should wait a while yet. They were relieved nonetheless when Netta took it upon herself to investigate, then scared when she reported back that she had found the door locked and had got no response when she knocked and called.

Bella started to warm up for one of her panics: 'Oh my God, what's happened? You'll need to break the door down, oh my God.'

'Aw right, aw right, keep the heid.' Already Phil was rolling his sleeves up for business. 'Come on we'll see.'

They went, all five of them, with Phil at the front and John at the rear, resolutely along the landing to the lavatory. Phil strode out masterfully enough, firm in his authority as head of the family, but as he turned into the recess a sudden shyness, a sudden doubt whether this was, in fact, man's business, drew him up short.

'Bella, gie that door a chap,' he commanded.

Bella was horrified. 'Not on your life. You dae it.'

'I cannae dae it, for Christ's sake.'

'Well I cannae either, so there.'

'Come here, I'll dae it,' Netta said, stepping between them. She rapped on the door with her knuckles, then thumped it with her palms, and called out, 'Jacqueline! Jacqueline! You in there? You aw right?' She stopped. 'It's nae use – she must have fainted or something. You'll need to look through the keyhole.'

'Aye, Phil, so you will,' said Bella.

Phil took a deep breath before he attacked. This was clearly *not* men's work.

'Jesus Christ, you expect *me* to do that? You kidding? Jesus Christ, what do you think this *is*?'

'Well somebody'll need to dae it, won't they? She cannae lie in that place all day.' Netta, as she spoke, was already looking at John, and the others picked up the hint. It seemed somehow less shocking for a child. John was willing enough.

'Aw right, well – but you said I could, mind.'

'Aye, come on now – see if she's still in there,' said Phil.

He stepped forward, bent, put his eye to the keyhole, said nothing.

'Is she there, for Christ's sake?' said Phil.

'Just a minute, will you? The key's in the door, you cannae see right, just a wee space. It's awful dark in there.' Jacqueline had turned the key sufficiently to leave a sliver of space, but the lavatory was dark, and in the general panic and his own private excitement he had difficulty in piecing together the puzzle, in making sense of the little that could be seen. He stared first with his left eye, then switched to his right. And suddenly it leapt at him.

Whiteness. Reflecting the dirty light, detaching itself from the murky backdrop, the girl's exposed whiteness. She had slipped from the bowl, turning as she fell, and had finished crumpled and prostrate before the porcelain, in the attitude of a praying muslim, with her head resting on her hands, and her legs folded under her and her bottom raised towards the door.

'Oh help,' John said, almost under his breath.

'What is it? Is she aw right?'

'She's fell aff the pan. She looks deid, kind of.'

This was too much for Bella. She grabbed Phil by the arm and started fainting procedures.

'Oh what'll we dae, Phil? We'll need to get a key.'

'A key's nae use, stupit – she's got our key stuck in there,' he said.

He cleared the others away and positioned himself for a kick at the door. As he drew his foot back, John said to Netta, 'Her knickers are aw doon – you can see her bare bum.'

'Shut up, you – that's scandalous, so it is.' Netta was enjoying herself now. Overhearing them, Phil lowered his foot again.

'Oh Christ,' he said.

'What is it?' asked Bella.

'I cannae go breaking the bloody door down if the lassie's . . . if she's . . .'

'You'll need to break it down, but. There's bugger all else you can dae, is there?'

He pondered his options. 'Right. But you'll need to go in and make her . . . make her right.'

He was a fat strong man: one kick was enough to break the catch of the lock. He pushed the door fully open and stood primly back to let the women go in first.

'Right then?' he said, carefully averting his eyes. 'Is she aw right?'

'OK,' said Netta, who had done most of the work of making the girl decent.

She was beginning to stir, and as they helped her to her feet she mumbled, like a child having a bad dream.

'There now, you're aw right, hen, you're fine now,' Phil

said as he cradled her in his arms. He carried her back to the house and laid her on the bed. Her mumbling grew slowly more coherent, and in ten minutes she was able to sit up and tell her story.

'I'm awfully sorry, I really am, it was daft of me. I just thought . . . I don't know . . . the place was that big . . . I felt as if there was somebody in there . . . and then I couldn't see the door . . . and I just . . .' She began to cry, losing her words in heavy sniffing sobs of relief, laying her head on Phil's fat warm chest and letting the tears gush.

'The Man With The White Sandshoes,' John whispered, as Alastair showed him a secret warning fist and Netta, torn between real sympathy and a certain pleased scorn, tried not to laugh.

'Oh I'm awful awful sorry,' Jacqueline said, and began to dab her nose with a tiny flowery handkerchief. 'You'll think I'm that stupid.'

'Not at all hen – you're no the only one that's had a fright in there – that's a horrible place, that lavvy.' Phil had his thick arm round her shoulder. 'There's half the people up this stair feart to go near it, so they are.'

'It's full of ghosts,' John added, to general annoyance, but Jacqueline was recovering her poise now, and able to laugh a little at this.

'Oh, I just feel that stupid. Did I faint or something?'

'Out like a light,' said Phil, jollying her. 'Out like Max Schmelling. Good job naebody else was needing.'

Jacqueline finished her tea, though it was cold now, and Alastair, eager to get out, fetched her handbag. They left for town and behind them was palpable relief, mixed with amusement and the first hints of exaggeration that would elevate the story of Jacqueline and the closet into a fully embroidered legend.

For John, there remained an unforgettable image of frail whiteness and a worrying thought which he offered as his closing remark in the family discussion:

'If she disnae come back I won't get free passes for the zoo.'

Wullie and Billy

Wullie Moore did constant nightshift at the forge, from ten every night till ten the following morning, with time-and-a-quarter for the last two hours. He travelled to and from the forge on the No. 8 tram.

Each morning when he got off the tram at the Friar Street Gushet he crossed the road to the pub corner and joined the men who hung around there. A silent man, he made desultory shy contributions to their discussions of football and filmstars and the war, lent one or two hard-up members the price of a pint, and went into the pub when it opened at eleven. He drank two small bottles of Aiken's Pale Ale, supplemented on Fridays by two halves of Johnnie Walker. At twelve he left the pub and went up to the second house, third landing, where Mary had his dinner ready. On Monday it was stew, Tuesday mince, Wednesday scrambled egg (which he could hardly stomach), Thursday corned mutton, Friday fish, Saturday gigot chops (his favourite). Sunday he stayed in bed with his *Beano* books and there was soup.

He finished his weekday meals before one, when Dom his youngest got home from school, then went to bed. The house was quiet at dinner-times now because his grown-up children had their meals elsewhere.

Poor Wullie, the other tenants called him; Poor Old Moore, his wife; Poor Father, his eldest daughters; and Poor Old Da, Ena, young Mary and the two boys. Nobody really knew why he was Poor: he was silent, true, but a man of some presence, a leathery strong handsome man you felt you could turn to; a man who was always in work, and a sober man who let nothing take him past his self-decreed limit. Yet he was liked and pitied by everyone – the adults who had grown up with him and the children for whom he was a rarely-seen, almost never-heard thing of mystery. The workday ration of conversation between Mary and him was hardly ten words, but on Sundays the whole family lay in late and Mary slipped back into bed with him after lighting the gas under the soup and they sometimes talked.

Mary, a happy woman, had a reddish mark on her face, under the right cheekbone. Usually it was dormant and barely perceptible, but on the rare occasions when she grew hot and bothered it would flare up like a beacon. They called it her birthmark, and they were not far wrong: it was Wullie's mark, printed by his shy forehead over one-and-a-half thousand Sundays and, in earlier times, over some weekdays too. It was not even every Sunday now, but Mary was happy. The soup safely bubbling, she would slip out of her Paisley-pattern overall and climb back through the curtains of the bed-recess, rousing him. Thirty years sweating in the sulphurous depths of the forge had taken their toll, of course, and there were Sundays when the rhythmic rubbing of his head on her spot was almost the only sensation she was aware of. But she liked the pulse of it and she liked especially when, happily spent or resignedly unable, he hugged her hard and said 'Mary', and she tightened her clasp and said 'Wullie', adding in her head 'Poor Old Moore'. Then they would sleep clasped together for an hour before she got up to taste the soup.

Wullie had six *Beano* books, originally Dom's, and every Sunday he read them twice each, in an unvarying cycle. There were also a few *Dandys*, but these he only dipped into, usually for Desperate Dan. He was not a strong reader, and had to mouth the words silently and use his finger as a pointer. With the more difficult ones, though he had read them hundreds of times, the effort was such that they sometimes escaped audibly from his lips and slipped through the bed-curtain. His daughters, hearing a disembodied low 'med-i-cine' or 'ex-cell-ent' or 'mis-chiev-ous' from the recess, would collapse with laughter and Ellen the eldest would shake her head slowly and roll her eyes to the ceiling and say 'Poor Father!'

There was one friendship in Wullie's life: a strange little thing it was, and the forging of it was one of the tenement stories.

Billy was the daftest of all the daft things in the Road. He appeared on the first day of every school holiday, early in the morning, at the Gushet tramstop. And all day every day, with breaks for meals when his aunt came to fetch him, he watched the trams. At each No. 8 he jumped up and down on his toes, desperately and shortsightedly squinting through the windows.

His story was well known: his dog, Lassie, had leapt into a No. 8 tram and been borne into the innards of the city, never to return. This had happened, the children said, 'years and years ago', though Billy was hardly eight when he first took up his bouncing vigil. His arrival at the stop was one of the markers of holiday time, and always before he had been bouncing more than half-an-hour, word would have spread and the children would have gathered for their sport.

In the table of imbecility he was unchallenged at the bottom: even young Jessica the Dogbiter and Davey the Dumptruck played their parts in making fun of him. The most tireless of the Billy-baiters, though, was Wee Pete Simpson, whose legs were bent and perpetually brown. Thin and limited in their invention, and perhaps a little touched with guilt, the others were pleased enough to adopt Wee Pete's proposals and to fashion them into rituals, though they knew too well that Pete himself was a thin cat's whisker this side of half-wittedness.

So with the tonsils game. Billy, asked to show his tonsils, would fumble with his buttons and offer his silly little dickiebird for their ardent inspection. He would eat cigarette packets from the tramstop basket, rubbing his belly and mumbling 'Yummy-yummy' when he swallowed a Players packet because Wee Pete had told him these were especially tasty. His word-hoard was restricted to this and a few tirelessly repeated phrases – 'Lassie come home', 'Here comes the No. 8', and, enigmatically, 'My big auntie across the sea in Canada.'

John Findlay was Wee Pete's closest contemporary and best pal. Influenced by Michael Connolly, his uncle from the fourth storey – a gentle frail man with TB who foolishly and fatally clung to his job at the saw-mill – he was constantly ill at ease about the mocking of Billy, but was too conscious of his own reputation as a softie and a spoiled brat to openly denounce it. Once, unusually alone at the tramstop with Billy, he had told him his name and coaxed him into mouthing it a few times; but later the same day he had looked in vain for a flicker of recognition in the bright empty eyes, for a twitch, even, of the thin blue lips towards the little syllable. Billy was in another galaxy.

The weather had been fine and unseasonably warm for the first few days of the Easter holiday. The children, never fewer than six or seven of them, had been in unbroken attendance at the tramstop and were becoming bored. It was Friday morning, Good Friday, and they had at last grown tired after a protracted bout of their simplest cruellest game – jumping in unison with Billy, raising and dashing his hopes at each No. 8 – and had lapsed into quietness, preparatory to drifting off in search of fresh amusements.

Scared of the silence, Alice Jackson invited Billy to show his tonsils and offered to show hers in return. She was eleven and already budding, and stupid enough to fulfil her promise, which caused a small stir of excitement and brought a new wildness to Wee Pete's eyes; but his curiosity was not to be satisfied, for Billy was as incapable of saying yes as he was of saying no, and before Alice could enlarge upon her offer, people had begun to queue at the stop, some of them casting looks of patent disapproval on the proceedings.

Now, fearful of losing his gallery as the children began to drift their several ways, Wee Pete found inspiration. He cried out suddenly, arrestingly, splitting the silence:

'Hey, listen. I've got a great idea! We'll play Calvaries and Indians and Billy can be John Wayne.'

Flushed with recent memories of *She Wore A Yellow Ribbon* at the Odeon, they loudly agreed, and they stayed, and Wee Pete was galvanized. In a flurry of instant genius, he ran through No. 7 close to the backcourt midden and emerged into the Road again carrying a broomstick with a garment dangling from its end – a tattered remnant of a thing worn by women to make themselves look neater in the bum: all hooks and ribs and little straps for holding up stockings. Excited by it, they cheered.

'Here Billy, here's your horse and your calvary hat,' said Wee Pete.

Billy was as beatifically uncomprehending as ever, but they had their sport now, and they soon had him decked out as John Wayne, with a blackened handkerchief around his neck, seated astride the broomstick, clasping it tightly in his nervous little fingers. He was game enough, or at least whatever fears might have tinged his little frown of puzzlement were far beyond their reading as they pushed and cajoled him.

'Tonsils, tonsils, a great big tonsil!' Alice cried, slapping the pole and laughing so hard she hurt herself. 'A great big long tonsil!'

Billy stood transfixed and grinning, with the pole sticking out at front and back. They whooped now, and danced around him as he stood in rigid bewilderment, frowning a little but never quite losing the idiotic saintly smile.

Wee Pete bobbed up and down on his stained rickety legs, waving the knicker-thing around his head and emitting a frenzied concoction of Tarzan-yodels and swear-words. Alice clumped about in a helpless jack-knife, clutching her ribs in real pain and foaming at the lips, eyes streaming, and green bubbles forming, bursting, and reforming at her nostrils. Shuggie, her twin brother, discovered that he could inflict blinding pain on Billy by kicking the pole whenever his war dance took him within distance, and Billy would respond with a look of witless searing agony, then of terror lest the broomstick should fall, then would reassert the silly eternal grin when he recovered control of it.

Two adjacent sons of the Reid tribe, Thomas and Donald, eight and seven years old, fearsome things with their char-black teeth and black curly hair and eyes invincibly askew, strove to outdo each other in wickedness. Thomas spat – big chesty green gobs – at Billy's feet, and Donald followed suit for a moment or two, then – his own refinement – darted his head in towards the centre and spat into Billy's hair. Billy's hands stuck resolutely to the broomstick and the smile never completely left his soft face as the loathesome green stuff began to seep below the hairline. The dance was in full flow now. Joan Reid of the withered left arm was mesmerically frozen, staring sightlessly ahead, waving her good arm like an inverted pendulum across her breast, dead to all the world, including the twitching smiling thing at the still centre.

John Findlay, finally surrending to the frenzy of it, gyrated and whooped and spat once, thinly, on the ground. He was the biggest there, and the cleverest, and knew the voices – had heard them clearly enough the few times he had lifted Mars Bars or chewing gum from Mr Buchan's shop and the many times he had listened to Michael Connolly's stories. But they were drowned now in Apache war-cries.

Wee Pete planted the rag on Billy's head. 'There's your calvary hat, Billy. Come on. Let's ride west.'

He made bugle-noises and smacked Billy's rump and set him off in little piggy-jumps along the pavement, with the pole scraping on the flagstones and the knickers flapping at his ears and the green spittle streaming down his cheeks; and the others, brought to a new pitch of madness, filed in behind, orchestrating their screams into a unified chant.

Billy picked up a war-cry from them, a jungle-chant which in his version became 'Hunga-hun-ga, hung-ga'. They pushed him and trailed him up and down a ten-yard stretch of pavement, and they sang:

Around her bum she wore some yellow knickers,
She wore them at her dinner and she wore them at her tea,
And if you ask her why the heck she wore them,
She wore them for her lover in the US Calvary.
Cal-var-ee, Cal-var-ee,
She wore them for her lover in the US Calvary.

The song, as they pounded up and down, gradually disintegrated, became a wordless chant, a yodel, a scream. Alice fell down and writhed on the pavement; the Reid brothers smothered Billy in spit and snarled and began to kick him; Wee Pete screeched forth in witless joy and rubbed himself between the legs. John Findlay too, watching the bespattered horse-soldier as the fear grew in the silly eyes and the skinny hands, still welded to the broomstick, began to tremble, and listening to the gurgling Alice, was madly astir in his crotch.

He shouted, tried to make words: 'It's really . . . it's really . . . CAV-al-ry, you mugs . . . it's really . . .'

The words died, and the world leapt and screamed and blurred . . .

'Hey, yous yins! Stop tormenting that boy!'

They were some distance from the tramstop, and the waiters there, like the idlers on the corner across the road, had seen no reason to meddle. But Wullie Moore, stepping from the No. 8 at twenty-past ten, Wullie who spent hardly fifty words in a day, was ready to use them now in a single pouring-forth.

He reached their dance in five quick strides and broke it, spilling his righteous anger among the shocked and frightened Apaches, threatening to kick their arses, to murder them. Mildly afraid of him at the best of times, they scattered and found safe distance, some running away altogether, the bolder ones like Wee Pete hanging back to await developments.

Wullie turned his attention to Billy.

'Come here, son, come on and we'll get that thing off you.'

He prised the stick from Billy's rigid fingers, then lifted the rag from his head and, seeing the hideous mess, shook his fist at the tormentors.

'You wee swines,' he shouted. 'You wee animals . . . you dirty wee Protestants!'

He took a rag from his dungarees pocket and began wiping the boy's face. For Wee Pete, standing with John Findlay at a secure fifty yards, bitter at the intrusion into his sport and resolved on having the last word, the game was not over yet.

'Gaun, you old nutter,' he shouted. 'You daft old bastit, you're worser nor he is, so you are!'

John Findlay, safely beyond the reach of the man's fist and of his invective, but stung by his love, gripped Pete's arm.

'Shut up,' he said, almost in a whisper.

'What? You scared of that old bastit? He's just a bampot, he's a nutter, he's a . . . he just lies in bed the whole day reading *Beano* books. Listen to this.'

He turned again to face Wullie, who had cleaned Billy's head and was cradling it against his chest.

'Hey you! You're a headcase, so y'are. My mammy says you're just a stupit old . . .'

John Findlay, standing close behind him, kicked hard. There were sharp things, metal or stone or both, in the trouser pocket and they hurt John through his thin plimsoll, but he drew back to kick again. Wee Pete was suddenly tearful.

'You lees alane, John Findlay, I'll tell my mammy on you, I'll get our Lily, she'll murder you.'

'Shut up.'

'Naw, I willnae, no for you, John Findlay.'

'Shut up.'

'You gonnae make me, well?'

John Findlay took him by the left wrist and twisted. 'Fucking shut up or I'll fucking break your arm.'

He released Wee Pete, who ran some way along the Road, distancing himself from both his enemies, and called out:

'You're a bastit, John Findlay, you're another bampot! I hate your guts, I hope you die, I'll tell your mammy you swore.'

John's foot hurt, and when he turned again to look at

Wullie and Billy still folded together outside Rankin's funeral parlour, everything hurt.

'Mr Moore,' he said, too quietly for Wullie to hear, 'I'm sorry, Mr Moore.'

He crossed the Road to the close. The house on the second landing was empty – his parents and brother and sister all at work – but he had his own key. He went upstairs to take off his shoe and examine his bleeding foot.

Wullie did not cross to the corner cronies. He led the boy by the hand across the Road at a point further up, to Mr Buchan's shop. For George Buchan the sight of Wullie Moore coming through his door was no less startling than if a full-feathered chief of the Cheyenne had done so.

'Gie the wean some sweeties, George, some chocolate, or toffee, or . . .'

George Buchan filled a paper bag and Wullie took the laden Billy back across to the tramstop, to his post.

'You staun there and look at the caurs, son. You like to look at the caurs, don't you?'

He gave Billy a last comforting pat, then turned to cross the road again. Billy, biting into his chocolate through the wrapper, stared adoringly at his back. Wullie did not join the men at the corner this time either. He went straight upstairs to the second house on the third landing. Mary was surprised.

'What's the matter, Wullie? Something happen at work?'

He did not answer.

'You're awfy early, the fish is no even on yet.'

'Ach, I'm no hungry the day, Mary.'

He sat down to pull off his boots. He took off his jacket and his dungarees and stood by the sink in his pullover and long johns, washing his face.

'Well, what is it, but? Did something happen at the forge?'

He dried himself, then went to the bed, drew open the curtains, and lay down on his back.

'Where's the boy – where's Dominic?'

'Him? He's away with Daniel the day, on the train. They'll no be back till six o'clock.'

'Come on in, hen – just for a minute.'

'You daft or something? It's only Friday . . . the fish . . .'

'Come on, hen, come on in.' She rinsed the bread-crumbs and the fish-smell from her hands and went to the bed. 'What is it, Wullie? You no well?'

'Lie doon. Just for a minute.'

She lay beside him in her place on the room-side of the bed. She was worried. 'What is it, Wullie? You're all shaking.'

He leaned up on his elbow, facing her, looking at her.

'Mary.'

She turned her head away, resting her left cheek on the pillow. He rolled across, shyly, and put his forehead in the hollow of her right cheek, on her birthmark.

'Mary,' he said.

'Wullie.'

Elsie

The O'Haras were a big family, and Big was their epithet – Big Sean the coalman, Big Elsie, Big Ellen, Big Plookie and Big Michael, or Sniffer.

Big Sean, when he was not delivering coal and briquettes, was smoking his pipe in the leather armchair by the fire and spitting. As his coalman's stoop had worsened, so his spitting had grown less precise, and the right side of the fireplace was permanently stained. A strangely featureless man because of his black face and the impenetrable Irishness of his speech, he was nevertheless regarded with respect and some affection, and his shy strength combined with geography – he was head of the house in the first door, first landing – to imbue him with something of an elder's status.

Elsie, his wife, was hysterical and fat and universally loved as a translator of the ordinary into the amazing. Her world was loud, anarchic, peopled with ghosts and stranglers and very little between. She screamed through it and fainted out of it at least twice a day. The fainting was bright and technicolour: no mere instant passing away, it was prefaced by shouts and hoots, wavings of arms and desperate searchings after words to explain her predicament. The lapse into senselessness came then as a blessed release: cessation of noise, sigh, collapse. One talked-about Friday night she accomplished it twice in the space of three hours.

The beginning was in the National Commercial Bank. She cleaned it three nights a week – was given, extraordinarily, a key to the front door and one to the broomcupboard in the bowels of the building. She had never been especially happy about being trapped in the echoing cavern of the bank (she was instructed to lock the door from the inside) and it was her custom to enlist one or two of the tenement children as company.

That Friday she found none and had to go it alone. She thought about not turning the key, then recollected the manager's stern injunction and reluctantly, listening behind in the act, twisted it in the lock.

Cleaning the upper area, with the comforting sounds of people and traffic and the tramcar sparks flashing on the ceiling, was carried out safely, if a little more slowly than usual. But panic began its slow inexorable rise when she turned to look at the green door. Behind this was nothing but emptiness and windowless silence. She switched on the lights and stood a moment at the open door, clutching her bucket in her left hand and mop in her right, summoning her courage for the descent. After a mere four steps the loneliness began to afflict her, and she felt already cut off from the Road, the people, the soothing rattle of the tramcars. A further six took her to the first bend in the staircase, marked by a little square landing. And as she heaved herself and her equipment around this, she saw the man.

He was on the stairs, ten steps below – had obviously been lurking behind the door – and was now moving down ahead of her. She saw him in a blurred instant as he ran across the next landing and made for the cellar. She dropped her bucket and mop and stood for a moment frozen with terror.

'Who's that?' she said. 'Who's that? I'll tell the polis.'

She heard him now, heard his furtive feet on the stone floor of the cellar, then – too much for her overwrought nerves – his small sly laugh.

She ran screaming upstairs to the green door. In the main hall of the bank, where communication with the outside world became a possibility again, she screamed louder. She reached the door to the Road and groped for the key, but in her terror she pushed it too far into the lock and was unable to turn it. She bellowed, invoked the Blessed Virgin, screamed again, kicked the door. Behind her, she heard the footsteps of the man as he climbed up from the cellar, and when the creak of the green door announced his arrival at the top of the stairs she sighed, leaned against the door, and slid sedately enough to the floor.

Her screams had been heard outside and the police were summoned from Kenny Street Station.

They had problems. Not only was the bank door locked, but Elsie had settled her great weight against it, and there seemed no way of opening it without causing her injury. They sent for the manager, Mr McGregor, who arrived with his keys and a worried look. There was talk of the fire brigades, of breaking into the bank by splitting a door or smashing a window; but Sniffer, her youngest, had arrived, and he assured them that no such drastic action would be necessary.

'My mammy always wakens up in about five minutes – she's aye fainting. You just slap her a bit and she wakens up nae bother.'

So they knocked gently at the door for a while, and Mr McGregor and PC McGlaughlin took turns at making reassuring noises through the keyhole. Their presence there had attracted a crowd, and the talk was of robbery and murder.

She came round after the promised five minutes and responded to Mr McGregor's instructions about how to turn the key in the lock. They eased the door open. Seeing the policeman and the manager and the assembled nosey-parkers, she recovered her awareness of the situation, and, with it, her terror.

'There's a man in the cellar,' she told them, breathless in her fear. 'He came up the stairs at my back.'

The crowd was restrained from pushing forward by young PC Blake while PC McGlaughlin drew his truncheon and strode across to the green door.

'Was he carrying any weapons?' he asked Elsie.

'He was awful quiet,' she said, 'and big.'

'Did he say anything?'

'Naw, he was just creeping about.'

PC McGlaughlin opened the door with professional caution, holding his truncheon at the ready. The staircase was in full light.

'Right, Jimmy,' he called down to the cellar, 'this is the police. If you're down there you better come up right now or you'll be in big trouble – do you hear me?'

The intruder, if he heard, was not disposed to reply.

PC McGlaughlin looked enquiringly at Elsie and she, recovering her composure, said, 'That's funny, I hope it wisnae just me and my stupit imagination.' The silence was biting. The policeman and the manager looked at each other, then hard at Elsie. The crowd picked up the message.

'False alarm, false alarm – just her imagination, the stupit hoor.'

They searched downstairs, found nothing. They asked her to retrace her steps, and PC McGlaughlin pointed out how the change of illumination from upper to lower bulb caused a shift in the shadow, which looked for all the world as if it was leaping across the wall. Elsie was enraptured, and asked if they might do the trick again. Again the leaping shadow.

She laughed. 'That's great that, i'n't it? It looks just like somebody was running across in front of you. Funny I never noticed that before. And it's that quiet, tae – it's like a ghost, so it is.'

Mr McGregor was still concerned about his vaults.

'Are you quite sure that's what it was you saw, Mrs O'Hara?'

'That's it, definitely. What a fright I got! I even thought I heard him laughing, I got such a fright.'

Then she laughed her own special screeching relief-laugh, and even Mr McGregor – disturbed and torn from his chess-game with his precocious son who by now would have had time to study the position and consolidate an already formidable kingside defence – even he was disarmed and unable to do anything except laugh with her and tell her she'd done enough for one night, she should go home now and pour a cup of tea and rest her weary legs.

The news travelled along the Road ahead of her, and Sniffer had told Big Sean the whole story by the time she got back to the first house, first landing.

Big Sean was in his chair, smoking his pipe, half-sleeping to the sound of the Light Programme.

'Whitninnemmogaadsaalthisabite, wumman?' he said, not raising his head. In thirty years of living with him she had never got beyond the flimsiest understanding of his language. Now she took in just enough to realize he wanted the full details, and she told him the story while he half-listened to the wireless and puffed on his pipe and spat at the fire. He did not interrupt, reserving his comment until the end, when she had finished her relief-whoop.

'Bliddy eejit,' he said, and spat on the mantelpiece.

John Findlay came down from the second landing for a Friday-night comic-swop with Sniffer. He set his bundle down by the doorstep and squatted beside it while Sniffer combed the house for comics. He began sorting his bundle, making first a pile of coloured Americans, and alongside a pile of black-and-white British. Then he subdivided the Americans: wars, cowboys, Superman, horror, funnies. His was by far the most comprehensive library in the tenement.

It was late, half-past nine, but he was allowed up because it was Friday. He heard Sniffer blundering about in the bedroom, then shouting through the kitchen.

'Hey ma! Where's they Superman comics I had, and they Batmans?'

'What?'

'Where's aw they comics I had?'

'Och, they're under the bed, son. I seen them this morning.'

'Well I cannae find them.'

'Well you're no looking.'

Pat MacKay came into the close and started climbing the stairs. He was mumblingly drunk, as he always was at half-past nine on a Friday, after ten minutes in the pub and one pint of heavy – a weekly miracle satirically admired and envied by the other men. Not a popular man, especially in drink, he had acquired the habit of conversing with himself in long mumbling incoherent arguments only snatches of which escaped to the outer world. Sometimes when they grew heated, these arguments, they would develop into open quarrels and his arms would flail about in a pantomime brawl.

Tonight, though, he seemed benignly disposed. The dialogue was low, amiable, strewn with lines from his favourite and only song, 'We will follow Celtic', and by comradely calls up the stairwell to the skylight.

John Findlay knew that Pat MacKay, however drunk and however contented, was not one to lapse into generosity on meeting a child on the staircase, so his interest was casual, and led him to pause in his business only when some colourful patches of dialogue stood out from the general blandness. Pat MacKay's progress was slow, punctuated with stops for breath, for salutations to the skylight, for clinching an argument or orchestrating a chorus.

'That's the game . . . you show them . . . bastits . . . mumblemumble . . . immaterial, imma-fucking-terial . . . see him? See him? . . . They're aw the same, the bastits . . . mumblemumble . . . King James . . . up the rebels! . . . Sort the bastits out, nae bother . . . nae torraborra . . . Hey! Hey Rosie! See ye, see ye the night, hen, see ye in the morning . . . anywhere The Celtic go we'll follow on . . . Follow, follow, we will follow Celtic, anywhere, up the stair . . . fucking Batman and Robin . . . wheeeee . . . !'

He stopped halfway up the first flight, leaned across the bannister, and shouted up the stairwell:

'Rosie, here I come! Batman and Robin and Rabbie Burns . . . here I come, the star o' Rabbie Burns . . .'

He leaned too far, and his body buckled across the bannister. As it did so, his hand was already reaching out to take hold of the iron bar that ran from the edge of the first landing across and down to meet the staircase opposite. His feet lost contact with the stairs, his left hand gripped the bar beside his right, his body and legs slid across the railing, swung through a half-circle, and he was dangling from the bar, swinging apelike in the dark void above the close. He seemed undistressed by the arrangement, and pleased with the view it afforded him of the stairwell.

'Rabbie Burns!' he called to the distant skylight, 'Rabbie fucking Burns.' Enjoying the echo, and inspired by his exciting and unwonted Tarzan-view, he found and gave full-blooded voice to another song:

Let kings and empires rise and fall,

This world has mony turns,
But brightly shines aboon them a' . . .
The star o' Rabbie Burns.

It was this new element, this unfamiliar song, that roused John Findlay. There was no sense of crisis: he noted that Pat MacKay had disappeared, and went to the bannister to investigate. He saw Pat, dangling by one arm now and mumbling.

'Are you aw right, Mr MacKay?' he asked.

Pat mumbled a little louder, then burst into a chorus of 'We will follow Celtic'.

At first mildly hypnotized by the sight of the man swaying gently in the void and by the sound of his crooning, John simply watched. Then he noticed the face slowly reddening, and the voice taking on a strained grunting quality that argued some difficulty in maintaining the position.

He went back to the O'Hara door, which stood a little ajar. He could hear Elsie rummaging under the bed, helping Sniffer to look for his comics.

'Eh, Mrs O'Hara?' he said quietly, then louder when she failed to respond. 'Mrs O'Hara? I think Mr MacKay needs help – he's fell ower the bannister.'

'What's that, John son?'

'Mr MacKay – he's hinging fae that railing thing.'

Elsie came to the door, frowning. 'Where is he, the silly bugger?'

She walked to the bannister, looked across, and screamed.

'Oh my God! Oh Jesus! Oh Holymarymotheragod! Oh Jesus our saviour in Heaven! Oh Sean, oh Sean, oh Sean!'

It was the saving of Pat MacKay's bones that instant unconsciousness was not her style. She ran back into the house and shook Big Sean, then pulled him from the chair that he would never have vacated for a mere scream. Neighbours had been roused, and were beginning to appear on the bannisters above, leaning across in happy expectation of some wild continuation of Elsie's night of adventure. Big Sean reached Pat first, followed by the bullet-figure of Bumpstead Ruskin from the fourth house. Strong men both, they soon managed to take firm hold of Pat and drag him across the bannister to safety.

The pub had disgorged now, and several of the other men had come into the close.

'What's the matter with that daft bastit?' Willie Jackson asked, and without waiting for an answer went on, 'Christ, do you know what he's had down there? One pint! One measly pint of heavy! I watched the bastit.'

They did know, because Pat had never to anyone's knowledge drunk more or less than one pint during any of his ten-minute sojourns in the pub. But neither he nor they could tell if his drunkenness was real or feigned, and neither he nor his wife Rosie knew whether his tales of gallons of beer and whisky with which he entertained her and maintained his manhood every Friday night were real or imagined.

He was helped upstairs to the third landing. Elsie did not follow the crowd, but stepped past the boys, who were busy negotiating the exchange of comics on the doorstep. Sniffer, with her help, had unearthed some battered Britishers, and John was quoting, cruelly, a price of three for a good American horror.

'That's no fair, Johnnie boy,' said Sniffer, snorting with indignation and drawing his sleeve across his nose in a gesture of righteous anger. 'It's two British for a Yank.'

'Aye, but yours are aw torn, Michael, and mine are like new.'

'Och, have a heart, I've only got these six – gies three of your Yanks for them and you're a pal for life.'

John, conscious of Sniffer's own generosity when he was in funds, relented. Sniffer was ecstatic about his bright new acquisitions and went into the bedroom to look for some more hidden Britishers.

'Oh naw,' he said.

He came back to the doorway, empty-handed, just as Big Sean arrived back from the third landing.

'Hey Da,' he said, clapping his hands to the top of his head and rolling his eyeballs. 'My mammy's fainted again.'

Thomas D. Forsyth

I'm the man from the Water Department, ho, ho, ho. Got a wee card: Thomas D. Forsyth (that's my real name, ho, ho). Assistant Chief Supervising Engineer, Water Department. I've never had to show it yet, they let me in as soon as they see my face. Mr Reliable, that's me.

Hang about for a day or two, watch the men, watch the women, talk to the kids, into action.

'Excuse me, son, is that Mr O'Hara's (the nameplate's quite a nice bit of brass) house?'

'Aye, but he'll be in his bed just now, mister, he's been on the early run.'

'Excuse me, hen, is this Mr Sloag's house?'

'No, that's just old Mrs Sloag – she lives by herself.'

Very interesting. No bother at all.

That No. 30 was a laugh, but it wasn't worth the sweat. Cheapskate bastards. Dead easy, they don't hide things, keep their purses in the side-board drawer, or just lying on the top. The kid in the first house kept watching me, but I sent her ben the room to listen to the pipes, then I whipped the mother's purse into my wee black bag. (Wee, that's a laugh, you could put the crown jewels in it, no bother at all.)

My god. The purses were worth a damn sight more than what was in them, but it was a good laugh.

'Good morning, I'm from the Water Department. We hear you've been having some trouble with your supply lately.'

'You mean that bloody chipshop?'

'Eh yes.' (In like lightning.)

'It's bloody terrible. That wee swine Freddy does it deliberate, he runs all the watter so naebody else can get any.'

'Mm, I see. Can I just take a wee look?'

So in I go, up to the sink, out with the pliers. Rap, rap, turn on the water, rap, rap.

'Mm.'

'Is there something the matter with it?'

'Mm. Where's your toilet?'

'Upstairs, on the second storey.'

'Mm. (Rap, rap.) I wonder . . . do you think you could maybe just nip up and flush it for me? I have to listen to the distribution.'

'Right, I'll not be a minute.'

One purse, one gent's wristwatch.

The old dear in the third house was too weak to climb the stairs, but she was half-blind anyway. She had a smashing fat purse, but it was just a load of old birth certificates and things, as it turned out. (The joke was on me for a change, saves me getting too big-headed.)

It got easier the higher I went – their supply was even worse, so they were really glad to see me. I had loads of time on the first and third landings. They had to go up the stairs to the toilet.

Christ, I nearly die laughing when I think of it. A whole morning, a whole procession of stupid women, in and out of those toilets like yo-yos, pulling the plugs like bampots. It's a wonder the chains didn't break. Bet their men killed them when they got back, bet they called them silly bitches.

My wee black bag was bulging: eight purses, four watches, a pile of pennies meant for the gasman, a mother-of-pearl lighter, two cigarette-cases, a silver locket, three nice books. I opened the purses in the Cuddies Park and I nearly swore. A load of copper it was – less than four quid all told, for a morning's work. But I fancied the doll in the first house on the top landing, Mrs Connolly. She said she works shifts at the telephone exchange. Nice bit of stuff – and she said she likes a good laugh.

Usually I'm nice, I stick all the empty purses in a poke and leave it somewhere handy, in the close or something – no skin off my nose. But this time I was so aggravated I just flung the lot in the Stinky Ocean.

Cheapskates. But I might go back to that top landing, one of these fine days.

Pleasure

It was daft that a man whose legs hardly fitted should be living on the top landing and daft he should be on his own and the social work people should never come to see him, but there were plenty of other things just as daft, so nobody complained and Tam Burke was as happy as the next man.

He was well served by the women of that landing – plump sexy Margot Connolly flirted with him and big-hearted Jessie Brass, unabashed by the raw nakedness of his stumps, bathed him and dressed him and made meals for him and hugged him when he got depressed, and even the rattlesnake Lily McCaffrey did his shopping for him twice a week. Their men allowed it because Tam Burke played the banjo and was only three feet tall with his legs off.

He had been one of the few men who had been an age for war service and had not managed to get himself into a reserved occupation, and he had done his bit unheroically but steadily enough in North Africa before his legs went – not riddled with Nazi bullets, alas, but under a runaway lorry in Aldershot. They brought him back to the second house, fourth landing where his mother had died three months earlier and they dropped him into an armchair in his wooden legs and forgot about him.

The air raids were pretty well finished by that time, but when there was an alarm Michael Connolly and Alan Brass would carry him dangling from their necks by his strong arms down to the shelter. He only wore his legs on special occasions because they hurt him and made him feel dizzy.

Most evenings he strapped them on to clatter down to the pub with his banjo, but once he was settled in his corner with his pint and his Johnnie Walker Black Label he would slip them off and lay them under the table. Music and singing were strictly barred, but because he had no legs he was allowed to strum a little and give the odd chorus of 'The Cowboy's Wedding Day' or 'The Wild Side of Life'.

The legs never stayed where he left them. At some point in the evening somebody would pick them up and they would be tossed about the pub and made the subject of endlessly repeated bad jokes:

'Hey, Mary, fancy a leg ower?'

'Whit? Don't be cheeky, you dirty-minded bastit, I'll tell my man on you.'

'Naw, no that – a leg ower the table (throwing one of Tam's legs across). It's you that's the dirty-minded one.'

And at half-past nine, when George Thompson announced closing time, Tam would look under the table and say, 'Christ, where's my legs got tae this time?' And they would say, 'Never mind your legs, come on we'll get you up the stair.' And two of the men would be detailed to carry him and his banjo up to the fourth landing while the rest looked for the legs.

On Saturday nights they bought screwtops and half-bottles and continued the revelry in one or more of the houses where they could join in the chorus and he could play as loud as he liked. Then on the Sunday morning the youngest mobile child of whatever house the legs ended up in would rap on his door and shout, 'Mr Burke, my mammy says here's your legs.' And Tam would call the child in and give it sixpence, and when it had gone he would strap the legs on and switch on the wireless and dance a bit, just to check they were still working. They worked fine, but he always got them off again before Big

Jessie came with his soup at dinner-time. She had to find him legless and gently depressed, listening to *Family Favourites* and getting maudlin about the war and about his dead mother and even, if he felt another turn of the screw was needed, about Tammy Burke, his dead father, who had passed on unloved and unlamented when his only child was just six. She liked him like that.

Over his three women he exercised a benign and total tyranny. He never complained, or whined, or raised his voice, or issued commands: a hint of a hint to one that her ministrations fell short of those provided by the others was enough.

Differing completely in their styles, they were one in their dedication to his comfort and happiness. Lily McCaffrey, as she unloaded his provisions, came nearer to gentleness with him than she did with any other living creature. Margot Connolly dressed up to visit him three mornings a week, and sat long enough to share ten Capstan with him, and titillated him with exaggerated stories of her weekend adventures, and ruffled his hair when she left. Sometimes she planted a lipstick-print on his cheek.

It was tacitly accepted, however, not only by these two but by all the rest of the tenement, that Big Jessie was his special love. Every Sunday she set the zinc basin in front of the fire, emptied the kettles of hot water into it, tested the temperature with her elbow, and helped him in. Leglessness legitimized – turned a thirty-seven-year-old woman and a man just six years younger into mother and child; and shamelessly he let her rub him all over with Lifebuoy, and dry him and powder the painful parts where his legs chafed.

Generous to the children, unleashing the mother-instincts of the women, posing no threat to the men, and entertaining all of them with his music, he was well enough liked in the tenement, except by Bumpstead Ruskin, who craved the skilled motherly hands of Big Jessie for himself. Spurned a dozen times and cold in his loveless bed, he found it rankling to the point of sickness that Tam Burke should effortlessly and for the mere loss of two legs have won the most coveted of prizes. And thoughts of revenge plagued him in his headlong rushes around the block and up and down the stairs.

Jessie fell stupidly in love with The Man With The Painted Heid, but she did not let her passion interfere with her attentions to Tam Burke. It was that passion, though, that brought about the final translation of Bumpstead's evil thought into evil action.

The pub was chockablock on a wet Saturday night, and George Thompson, his mood softened by a bulging till, let them sing along with Tam until the ceiling shook with the din of it. Bumpstead took up his customary position at the bar, close by but with his back to the window-seat where Jessie and The Man With The Painted Heid held court. The Man With The Painted Heid had his arm around Jessie's shoulder, and was furtively squeezing her right breast with his fingers and openly kissing her about the head and ears. And while the whole crowd of them riotously assisted Tam with 'The Cowboy's Wedding Day', Bumpstead dipped his head and squinted over his left shoulder at The Man With The Painted Heid's impudent and welcome fingers, and felt his stomach churn with bitter rage. The song finished, and Tam fished out some more applause with some fancy chords before drowning his Black Label.

While they waited for the next number, Bumpstead could listen to the conversation at the table. Caught up in the noise and music and fellowship, Jessie relaxed and, lapsing from her usual discretion, joined in their talk about the minstrel.

'He's a rerr wee singer,' said Willie Jackson.

'Aye,' Jock Simpson agreed.

'Great how he does it,' Willie went on, 'haunling that big banjo.'

Jessie, her nose pressed against the Man With The Painted Heid's cheek, snorted with laughter.

'Big banjo?' she said, stressing the second syllable suggestively. 'You can say that again. He's got the biggest banjo I've ever seen!'

The others laughed, and she patted The Man With The Painted Heid on the top of his cap and added, 'And that's saying something, isn't it darling?'

He blushed with pleasure, and the others, egging her on, laughed till their sides ached.

'Big's no in it,' she hooted. 'I use a hale bar of soap washing it every Sunday, so I dae.'

They roared, and slapped the table, and cried on each other's shoulders.

'Nae kidding, it's like that bloody flagpole on the tap of the City Chambers,' she said finally, while they choked on their drinks.

Eaten with rage and unable to listen any longer, Bumpstead Ruskin left his pint on the bar and stormed into the toilet. He went into the cubicle and locked it and stood over the bowl. Leaning his head against the cistern pipe and closing his eyes, he let the hideous images Big Jessie had conjured up stir in his skull until he felt dizzy and had to take hold of the pipe to keep himself upright.

'Fucking fucking fucking bastits, fucking perverts,' he said, and vomited into the bowl. He flushed it, closed his eyes again, and leaned his head against the soothing coolness of the pipe. He felt altogether cooler, purged.

He opened his eyes and turned to go, and saw, propped up in the corner beyond the door, Tam Burke's right leg. He lifted it, enjoying the surprising weight of it and suspending his malice long enough for his handyman's eye to admire the quality of the carpentry. He thought about smashing it against the wall, then noticed the open ventilation light high up under the ceiling. He climbed on the bowl, and by bending the leg at a convenient angle, was able to push it through to the backcourt. Hearing it drop on the dirt, he muttered, 'Fucking bastits,' and, his step light and purposeful, went through the pub door into the night.

Although it was hardly nine o'clock, Soorpuss, his wife, was in bed when he got back to the fourth house, first landing.

'That you, Bumpstead?' she called from the recess.

'Shut up,' he said. 'Go tae sleep.'

He took his saw from under the bed and using the wooden fireside stool as a saw-horse he cut Tam Burke's right leg into pieces small enough for the fire. Guilt and the fear of discovery made his heart pound while he worked, but as he warmed his hands in the yellow glow of the last piece he felt himself suffused by a long-lost sense of calm. He undressed and climbed into the bed beside Soorpuss and for the first time in five years slept the night through.

There was no undue panic at half-past nine when only the left leg turned up: people were enjoying themselves, and everybody knew that both legs were always there, reporting for duty, on Sunday morning. The party spilled from the O'Hara's upstairs to the Jackson's and finally to the Reid's on the third landing. At about three o'clock Jock Simpson and The Man With The Painted Heid staggered up to the top landing with Tam Burke asleep and dangling between them. They dropped him and his banjo into bed then sat on the floor to finish Jock's half-bottle.

'Hope the wee bastit finds his leg,' said Jock.

'Aye,' said The Man With The Painted Heid, with a benign burp. 'He's good company, the wee bastit, he's a good laugh.'

Wee Pete Simpson was worried when he turned up at the second door, fourth landing the next morning with only one leg to deliver, but Tam Burke was not one to deny the child his reward, and the full sixpence was handed over. Wee Pete went back downstairs hopeful of doubling his wealth by finding the fugitive limb.

When Big Jessie brought Tam his soup at dinner-time she found him even more depressed than usual.

'Nae sign of your leg, Tammy son?'

'Naw Jessie.'

'Never you mind – it'll turn up somewhere, it aye does.'

'Naw Jessie, I've got a bad feeling about that leg, nae kidding. I think I've seen the last of it.'

'Don't be stupit – you're just feeling sorry for yourself. Anyway, you can write to the Social and get yoursel another one.'

'Write tae they bastits? That's a laugh. They run that Social tae suit theirsels. Naw, I've had it, finished, scrubbed, full-time whistle – that's me a cripple for life.'

'Och shut up and eat your soup. You never wear the bloody things anyway, I don't know what you're moaning about. Look, there's big lumps of chicken in it, that was a smashing burd oor Maureen brought us yesterday.'

'Ta Jessie, it looks great.'

She went to the door. 'See you the night then, aw right?'

'Right, hen, right you are.'

As she was opening the door, he stopped her. 'Jessie!'

'Whit? You wanting merr salt?'

'You're awfy good tae me hen, awfy awfy good.'

Sentimentality was not Big Jessie's cup of tea. 'Shut your face, stupit, I'll see you the night,' she said.

Throughout the day, visitors called and enquired about

his leg and proffered sympathy and left presents: Rich Tea biscuits, sugar, cigarettes, war-stories, a quarter-bottle of Red Hackle. By nine o'clock, when Big Jessie arrived to get the bath ready, it was clear that the leg was seriously missing. There were murmurings about foul play and dirty tricks, and Bumpstead Ruskin's name was cited more than once. But his perfidy had gone unwitnessed.

The torrents of sympathy had had their predictable effect, and Big Jessie found him tearful. She set about the business in hand with her usual vigour, ignoring his whinings till she had him safely stripped and propped up in the bath.

'Oh Jessie,' he bleated. 'Whit'm I gonnae dae? An old cripple wi one wooden leg?'

'Whit dae you mean, whit you gonnae dae? Same's you've aye done – doon tae the pub and drink yourself stupit and play your banjo and your Auntie Jessie and Big Margot and Wee Lily'll look eftir you, same as always.'

'Oh yous are good tae me yous girls, really good tae me.'

'Bloody dead right we are.'

'But you're the best, Jessie, nae getting away fae it. I'm no saying nothing against Margot and Lily, but you're definitely the tops.'

'Oh aye,' she said, lathering his scalp.

'You're the wife I never had, Jessie, and a mother forby. I don't know whit I'd dae withoot you, I really don't. You're just like my mammy used tae be, God rest her.'

'Watch you don't get soap in your eyes.'

'A pure mother – you spoil me rotten, Jessie.'

'Shut up and lift yoursel a bit – I cannae get the sponge under you.'

'Aye Jessie, I don't know whit I'd dae withoot you – especially noo I'm a one-leggit cripple.'

'Christ, will you shut up aboot that cripple? It's no the end of the world.'

'But it is, Jessie – a man wi one bloody leg, and that's a stupit wooden thing!'

She was washing his belly now, supporting his back with her broad left forearm while she held the sponge in her right hand and cleaned him with firm rhythmic strokes.

'That's lovely, hen, you're that good tae me, you'll get your reward in Heaven wi my dear mother,' he said, letting a small tear trickle down each cheek.

'Listen, just shut your face and lie back a bit and I'll sponge you the way you like it.'

She began to stroke him with the sponge softly, knowingly, cunningly, the way he liked it, and he shut his eyes and held tight to the edges of the bath.

'There noo,' she said. 'There, there, just lie back and let your Auntie Jessie look eftir you.' She was smiling, now that he could not see her face, enjoying her own cleverness as she coaxed his gently floating member up out of the foam. 'Here's wee MacTadger coming up to say hello.'

'Oh Jessie, you're good tae me.'

'There, there.'

'Oh Jessie.'

At half-past nine she stopped and picked up a towel.

'Right well, time I was away. My man'll be wondering whit's happened tae me. Come on we'll get you dry.'

'Aw Jessie, just a wee bit merr, just a bit.'

'Not on your nelly – you've had your ration.'

'Aw Jessie, I'm that depressed.'

She dropped the towel.

'My God,' she said, 'I don't know whit my man would say if he seen this. Shut your eyes.' And not using the sponge now, but only her clever motherly fingers, she soothed away his self-pitying sorrow.

Lily McCaffrey, bringing his shopping on the Monday

morning, was wickedly sympathetic. She had been in the pub on Saturday and had listened as eagerly to Big Jessie's dissertation on banjos as Bumpstead Ruskin, and almost as bitterly. Despite her curiosity, an obscure sense of grievance had kept her from visiting the stricken one on Sunday. Now, in the Monday morning hour that she knew was exclusively hers, she found her customary bluff solicitude reasserting itself, but a little hardened by spleen.

Tam Burke was too absorbed in his own misery to note the edge of malice in her questions.

'You'd plenty of visitors yesterday, eh?'

'Aye, people are good.'

'Bet you they are. Was that Bella Findlay here?'

'Aye, she brought me some fags.'

'Helluvu hearty. And who else?'

'Oh Christ, nearly everybody – it was like Sauchiehall Street in here. And they aw brought me things, God bless them.'

'Oh aye. And whit did your big Auntie Jessie bring you?'

'Jessie? She gied me my soup same as she always does. She's a good soul, that Jessie. Her and Margot and you make my life worth living, so yous dae.'

'But especially her, eh? She's your favourite, i'n't she?'

'Naw, naw, Lily – yous are aw good tae me.'

'Come on noo, tell the truth – she's especially good, i'n't she? She gies you things naebody else does, doesn't she?'

'You're aw good Lily, hen. You get my messages, and Margot, she gies me fags and makes me laugh, and Jessie brings me my soup.'

'Aye – and the rest. It's no just soup, is it?'

'Naw, naw. She gies me my bath and she powders my stumps – she's a real mother tae me, that's the God's honest truth.'

'Bath, eh? You want tae have heard her in the pub talking aboot that.'

'When?'

'Saturday night, wi that bampot with the painted heid and aw their cronies.'

'Aw that. Christ, I heard that – that was just a laugh.'

'Aye, well it sounds as if she gets a rerr laugh anyway.'

'Och, don't moan aboot Jessie, Lily, she's a good soul.'

'You never ask me tae bath you.'

He frowned. 'Well naw, I don't like. It's no everybody can stomach it, some people are easy scunnered.'

'Whit dae you mean – your stumps?'

'Aye. Jessie's no up nor doon, it doesnae upset her.'

'Whit makes you think it would upset me, well?'

'It's no that, Lily. I just don't like.'

She went across the floor to him and knelt down by his chair. She had taken off her coat when she came in, and she was wearing a Monday-fresh white blouse, open at the neck to show her white throat and her deeply-hollowed collar-bones, and a tight black skirt that she had to ease above her knees for comfort while she was kneeling. She was a thin, bony, tense, electric thing; he could see the pulse in her throat. Her dark gypsy face would have been pretty, except that her scowl of contempt for the world had become a habit. She was leaning over him with her head a foot above his groin.

'Whit does that Big Jessie dae?'

'Whit dae you mean?'

'You know fine what I mean. Does she wash you doon there?'

'Aye.'

'Aw the way roon, in, oot, everywhere?'

'She's a good soul.'

'You should've heard whit she was saying aboot you on Saturday night.'

'I did hear her. I telt you, that was nothing, that was just a laugh.'

'Just a laugh was it? You mean it's no really like a flagpole?'

Faced with the lawyer's question, Tam could only stutter; but Lily's insistent nearness, and her nervousness, and her pulsing white throat, and her collar-bones, and the memories she stirred of the previous night – these things were not to be brushed aside.

'O-ho,' she said, bending till her nose almost touched his swelling. 'I see whit she meant, you dirty wee bugger.'

With the tip of her finger she scratched him lightly through the cloth of his trousers.

'Christamighty, Lily, whit you daeing?'

'Does your big Auntie Jessie no dae this?'

'Christ naw – she just washes me.'

'Are you sure?'

'Sure I'm sure. Honest tae God, she just washes me.'

'Does she no dae this?' she said, beginning to undo his buttons.

'Jesus, Lily.'

'My, my,' she said, 'so there's the wee flagpole.'

'Aye,' he said, for want of a better answer.

'Does she no dae this?'

'Christ, Lily.'

'Does she no dae this?'

'Oh Godamighty!'

'Whit dae you think of your Auntie Lily noo, then?'

'Oh God, Lily, you're good tae me, you're good tae me, you're awfy awfy good.'

Michael and Margot Connolly had been away for the weekend at Loch Lomond with Dan Lawson and a couple they had met the previous year on holiday at Blackpool.

Childless and both working, they were able to take off like this two or three times a year to escape from the crowd and meet a better class of people. It reminded them of their days camping and youth-hostelling before the war, though they stayed in hotels now.

Margot had looked in on Jane Simpson on the Sunday night when they got back home, to catch up on the gossip, so she knew about the missing leg and about Big Jessie's flagpole story. She was not due back at the telephone exchange till the late shift on Monday, so she lay in till nearly noon, then spent an hour or two making herself beautiful for the visit to Tam Burke, whose front door was less than six feet from her own. She went in at quarter-past two with ten Capstans and a quarter-bottle of Bells, and found him in his armchair with his war-stories.

'Hello wee man – am I interrupting anything?'

His delight in seeing her was apparent in the eagerness with which he dropped his book, in his bright smile, and in the way his hand went up to tidy his hair.

'Margot! Come in sweetheart – I've missed you.'

Familiarly she took two glasses from the sideboard and emptied the quarter-bottle, a liberal measure into each. She sat in the armchair opposite his, crossing her long legs and sipping his whisky before she spoke.

'Right then, young Thomas, give me your worries – I hear you've been having a rough time while I was away.' She used her telephonist's voice, because she knew he liked it and thought it gave her class.

'Oh Margot, Margot, it's been terrible, so it has, bloody terrible.' And he told her the story she already knew, and as he told it they drank the whisky and smoked the cigarettes and he worked himself yet again into a state of tearful self-pity.

'Don't upset yourself,' she said. 'We'll soon get you another leg.' She leaned across and patted him on the shoulder, and he bent his head so that his cheek could touch her hand.

'Anyway,' she went on, 'what's this I was hearing about you and Big Jessie having a carry on? Seems she was entertaining the whole pub with it.'

'Christ, no that again,' he groaned. 'That was just a laugh.'

'I see. Just a laugh was it?'

He was silent, and she kissed his nose. Her hair had been permed for the weekend, and was fragrant and wavy and brilliantly golden, and she was scented behind her ears, and scarlet-lipped, with her fingernails scarlet to match.

'I had a few laughs at the weekend as well,' she said, settling back in her chair again. 'Michael and Dan and I were at this hotel in Luss.'

'Oh aye, I hear it's awfy nice up that way.'

'Lovely. And we had this couple with us that we met last year in Blackpool – Eddie and Marie. They were a really good laugh.'

'That's good, hen, that's champion.'

'Yes, we had some really good laughs, especially one morning – what was it? – Saturday morning it must have been. You should have seen it. There was I, seven in the morning, slipping out of the bedroom, and what do I see in the hall but Eddie, tiptoeing to the gents, and near as dammit in his birthday suit. All he had on were these tiny wee underpants that hardly covered anything. I didn't know where to look, and neither did he!'

Tam laughed dutifully, but doubted if he was going to enjoy the rest of the story.

'But anyway, the real laugh came later, at night, when the bar closed and they came into our room for a drink. Eddie was trying to apologize and he said, "I thought it was too early to get caught, honest to God, I don't usually run about in public with just my drawers on." Then my Michael says, "What do you mean, just your drawers on? From what I heard it was just your drawers nearly off!" And we laughed and laughed and then Eddie touched me on the knee, and he said – dead quiet, you know? – "Listen, listen Margot, fair's fair, isn't it? I mean, you've seen me with my drawers nearly off so I've got to see you with yours nearly off. Am I right or am I wrong?" "Oh no you don't," says I, "it takes my man all his time to see that!" Well, we nearly died laughing, the whole lot of us, then I said, "But seeing as you're not everybody you can have a wee look – there you are." And I pulled my skirt up to just about there, just above my nylons, then down again quick as lightning. What a laugh it was.'

'Aye, sounds a rerr laugh,' said Tam. He was staring at the place where, a moment earlier, a white sliver of thigh had been exposed. 'I bet that made that guy's day for him.'

'What did?'

'That. Seeing your leg.'

'Don't be daft. He's been married fifteen years.'

'But I bet his wife's nothing like you.'

Margot was pleased. She said, 'No I don't suppose she is – she's a really skinny wee thing.'

'So that fella's seen something he'll no forget in a hurry.'

'But he only saw that much,' she said, pulling her skirt up again and this time leaving it an inch above her stocking-tops.

'Christ, Margot, you're a smasher – I wish I was a real man, instead of just a one-leggit cripple.'

'You *are* a real man. You're my wee pal.'

'Oh, but you're a smasher. Aw the men up here are mad aboot you.'

'Yes, all except you,' she said wickedly. 'You prefer Big Jessie.'

'Jessie? Naw, that's entirely different, that's no the same

thing at aw. Jessie's like a mother to me.'

'And what am I like? Am I just your favourite auntie?' Margot exaggerated her plummy telephone voice, teasing him.

'You're different . . . you're . . .' He put his glass down on the kerb, and almost knocked it over, his hand was shaking so much. 'Let's see a wee bit merr, Margot,' he blurted out.

'A-ah. Don't be cheeky. I'm a married woman.'

'Be a doll, Margot, I'm that depressed.'

'Are you well? There's one bit looks quite happy.'

He followed her glance. 'I'm sorry, I cannae help it, you're such a smasher.'

'Am I better than Big Jessie?'

'She's just like a mother tae me.'

'Am I better than Lily McCaffrey?'

'She just gets me my messages.'

'Well then.' She reached across to his buttons. 'I'll do you a wee favour, just this once, because you've lost your wee leg.'

'Jesus, Margot, you're good tae me,' he said, closing his eyes.

At half-past seven Jock Simpson and Willie Jackson, generously remembering Tam Burke's predicament, came to ask if he wanted carrying down to the pub. He was touched, but told them he wasn't feeling too great and was going to his bed early, for a change. They made sympathetic noises and went downstairs and for most of the night were George Thompson's only customers.

Tam's statement had been truthful enough. At nine he closed his book, shuffled across the floor on his hands and bottom to the armchair beside his bed, clambered in and put on his pyjama top. He lay on his back, staring at the ceiling, enjoying a sense of delicious exhaustion. He did not attempt to switch out the light because he was expecting Big Jessie to come soon on her bedtime inspection. When she arrived, about half-past nine, he was in a happy doze.

'You aw right, Tammy son?'

'Whit? Oh, that you Jessie? I'm fine, hen, marvellous, nae bother at aw.'

'You been worrying aboot your leg?'

'Naw, naw – I've been fine, honest.'

'Listen, I meant tae say I was sorry aboot that in the pub the other night – me and my big stupit mooth.'

'Aw that's aw right, doll, that was just a laugh.'

'You sure?'

'Dead sure, nae bother.'

'You're a wee sport, Tammy.'

'Anyway,' he said, sensing her guilt and inspired by a sudden flash of mischief, 'it was only the truth.'

'Whit you mean?' She was sitting on the arm of the chair, beside the bed.

'That aboot the flagpole. I mean tae say, there's no a lot of flagpoles roon this dump – we might as well bum aboot the ones we've got, eh?'

'Oh you cheeky wee messin!'

'Come on, tell the truth, doll, you've no seen many like that, have you?'

'Shut your face.'

They were quiet for a minute, sharing the happy memory. Then he made his move.

'You really were awfy good tae me, Jessie, I really mean it.'

'Aye, well, I said it was just the once.'

'But it was really good of you – I was that depressed.'

'I know. You were aggravated aboot your leg, it's only natural.'

'Aye.' He lifted himself on his elbows. 'I'm still a bit depressed.'

'Aw naw you don't!'

'I don't think I'll get tae sleep, Jessie. I just get these sort of like waves, these waves, they come across me, and I feel that miserable.'

'Look, we're no making a habit of this. My man would kill me if he knew.'

'I know, hen, I know. Honest tae God, just one last time, just tae get me tae sleep.'

'God, you're a right wee messin,' she said, pulling down the blanket.

In the pub George Thompson was pouring the last drinks, pints of heavy for Jock Simpson and Willie Jackson, a half-pint and a glass of Bells for Bumpstead Ruskin. Their conversation had turned to Tam Burke's legs, and Bumpstead's contributions had been desultory and even surlier than usual.

'Christ, you're awfy hard on the wee guy,' said Jock, after Bumpstead had dismissed Tam as a fucking loud-mouthed wee nyaff. 'I mean tae say he's no had a lot of luck.'

'That's right,' Willie agreed. 'He cannae get much pleasure oot of life, the way he is.'

'Hm,' said Bumpstead, thinking of his own bleak fireside, his cold bed.

'Naw,' said George, supporting their assault on Bumpstead's better nature, 'he cannae get a lot of pleasure.'

Upstairs, Big Jessie was leaving the second house, fourth landing.

'Noo remember – that's the very very very last time, right?' she called into the happy darkness.

'Right Jessie, right,' said Tam Burke. 'You're awfy good tae me, you're a real doll.'

My Tony

Oh, my Tony. He's a terrible man, they're right really, I suppose, he leads me a terrible life for all the fivers in his ears. I speak a bit better than the rest, they're a bit on the scruffy side. I was born in England and Tony goes down there quite a lot with the caravans so he's a nice speaker as well, that I will admit, he speaks like Al Jolson and sometimes he does James Cagney, that's really good, he should be on the stage with that, honest to God.

I've a terrible life with him really. He's nice when he's sober – well, that's what they all say, though how they know, it's a mystery to me. But one thing that is true, they say the wildness is in his blood, and God strike me down that is the truth sure as I'm sitting here. He's got a lot of style, like somebody in the pictures, he's been down in England a lot – and I've got some as well, I must admit. I've got very good taste, but I moan a bit and I throw things. I wanted to be near my cousin Bella – she's on the same landing, along at the other end, that's the reason we came here instead of buying one of those bungalows. I don't fancy those bungalows, I mean they look lovely, but it's more friendly here in the town. We got this place when Big Jessie and Alan Brass moved up to the top flat – she's living with that horrible foreign man now, him that paints his head with boot polish, God forgive her. There were really terrible things here when we moved in, you wouldn't believe it, there were dead rats in the presses and under the floorboards and the potato peelings were a foot deep in the bed-recess. Tony had loads of money then and I made the place really nice, though I say it myself. Everybody says it was like a miracle, what I did to this place. I love white, so I do. And I like contemporary.

I made the whole place white contemporary. The man came and took out the bed and converted the recess into a kitchenette – that cost me a mint, even the taps are white, and there's constant hot water. I got rid of that terrible old sink – I don't know how people can live with them, I really don't – and I put the television there, under the window. We were the first to get a television in the whole building, and we're the only ones with a phone, and the only ones with hot water. The bedroom door looks dangerous, but it's special glass – young Tony fell against it once and banged his head really hard on it but it didn't even break. The mural was the dearest of the lot, it cost me three hundred pounds, so it did. They all said I was daft, but it was a real artist and Tony likes it so that's good enough for me – they think you can get a real artist for sweeties and a balloon, some of the people up here. It was in a magazine, this bullfight picture, that Picasso drew it, so he did, it was just black and white and sort of, well, blotchy, and it was only a wee thing, but I got the man to copy it lifesize and make it sort of more real-looking and put in the background and make it coloured. It's lovely – I sit here and just stare at it for ages. Three hundred pounds – they thought I was round the bend, but it's a lovely picture, they have to admit that, it's just like being at the real bullfight.

Bella and I are awful like each other. We've both got ulcers, funny enough, and we've definitely got the same chin, everybody says that, but she's not a nice speaker, she's just like the rest of them up here. She thinks I'm daft for staying with Tony and maybe she's right, it's a terrible life sometimes.

You can tell I'm different just to look at me. I like to dress nice, even when I'm in the house. Last week the plumber came and I was in my Japanese dressing gown and he nearly died when I opened the door, he nearly dropped his toolbag, so he did. Tony's different as well. He's great with the women, I must admit, the men up here are all jealous of him, that's why they say he's just a layabout, but he's some layabout, he gets more money in a week than the rest of them put together get in a year, sometimes.

Tony's family are fair-ground people. I don't really know them, his mother's dead now. He goes with them whenever they're near the town and he sometimes goes down to England with them and he's away for weeks. That's when he comes back and if he's been lucky he's got fivers in his ears and he's singing that Al Jolson song, that 'Nothing Could Be Finer Than To Be In Carolina'. Sometimes he loses a lot on the horses, that's why I've got ulcers really, the doctor says it's worry, but he always seems to get more. I must admit he's nice when he's drunk if he's not *too* drunk. When he's sober he can hardly even talk, he can't even buy a packet of cigarettes, he gives one of the kids in the street a sixpence to go into the shop for him. Funny. When he's got just a little drink in him he's like Cary Grant, and he's a really lovely singer, everybody says that, even the men. He's got a lot of style, I must admit. Young Tony's just the same, he walks about clinking his money and jumps on and off roundabouts like a monkey, so he does. The other boys are all jealous of him, really really jealous.

Tony goes with women, I know that. They all think it's terrible and Bella says I should kick him out, but really, that's just My Tony, and as long as he doesn't bring them here and I don't see them, well, honest to God, if I was another woman *I'd* fancy him, I'd be chasing him same as they are, so why should I complain, he always comes back to me. Not that I don't shout at him. I shout and scream and break plates on him and funny enough, he never raises a hand to me. When he's been away for a while and I hear he's been seen in one of the pubs near here or maybe he's been up in that Skinny Lucy's house I just grab the children and go down the road to my mother's and he has to break the door down because he's never got a key. He's broken that door down three times already and we've only been here six months.

Louise is lovely, I must admit. She's like Tony and she's like me, but she's nicer than the two of us, if you see what I mean. She's not got my temper, thank God. She's only seven, but she's like a little angel, so she is, she's like Elizabeth Taylor, only blonde. They're all jealous of her up here, and they say I spoil her, but I think she deserves nothing but the best and that's what she'll get as far as I'm concerned. Her hair's lovely. I brush it and brush it right down her back and it really shines. She's like a little princess, she really is, especially when I dress her all in white. She's not like a child, really – she's a little lady. She never plays with the children up here except sometimes with Bella's boy, her cousin John. He's a bit nicer than the rest and he's really quite a nice speaker, funny enough. She's so different from young Tony, he's such a little devil, just like his daddy, every bit of him, even the way he talks. She's my little china doll, so she is.

Listen, I know I should have left him years ago and it's because of him I've got ulcers. I get so angry sometimes I get sick. I sit in the chair and I cry and cry and sometimes Bella comes in and she makes me a cup of tea and tells me I should leave him and she'll murder him when he gets back this time and he's nothing but a bad effer. But I make her promise not to say anything, and sometimes just to quiet her down I tell her I'll definitely leave him this time, he's gone over the score, he's finished as far as I'm concerned. But the thing is, just when I've decided that's it, finito, that's us finished, back he comes with the fivers sticking out everywhere and some really fancy present for me and that laugh of his and it doesn't matter how angry I am I'm really quite glad to see him and he says, 'Come on, give me a big cuddle baby, I promise I'll never do it again.'

I like cuddling him, I really do.

And my goodness, the presents he gives me. I could open a jeweller's shop, so I could – everybody says that. I was just showing my eighteen-carat bracelet to the women in the dairy last week. 'That's real gold,' says I, 'and real sapphires, what do you do with a man like that?' They nearly died when they saw the real sapphires. 'I know,' says they, 'he's an awful man, I don't know how you put up with him.' 'My Willie's just the same,' says Aggie Jackson, which is a real laugh because her Willie hasn't got two haepennies to rub together, neither he has. Then I took it off and showed them the inscription inside and they were just flabbergasted, they nearly died, so they did: 'I'd walk a million miles for one of your smiles my Mina' – all done in these lovely fancy letters, I nearly died myself when I saw it. What do you say to a man like that, I ask you, what do you say?

But there was one time, I must admit, just the one, when I really meant it, when I really went for his eyes, when I really said that's it, finished, get back to your gypsy relations and stay there. That was the day he opened the hair-dryer box.

We had our rules, you see, even though we never wrote them down. Tony could spend what he liked, he could throw it away if he liked, as long as he gave me enough for the housekeeping and never asked me for any of it back. And nearly always he stuck to that, he really did. He borrowed a lot from his cronies but he always paid it back and sometimes, very very occasionally, he would go really sweet and ask me, ever so nicely, for a fiver to see him through the week, and that was OK, that was nice, it would make him go quite romantic for a while and he would even kiss me in the road and the people here thought he was daft or something. But then this day came and he'd been good for ages and it was as if the strain was too much and he waited till I was out for some messages and then he raided the house and found one of my little hidey-holes. The trouble is I've never liked banks. It's maybe living with Tony that's done it, I don't know, I just don't feel happy unless I've got the money somewhere near me. So I've got these rolls of notes, fivers and tenners mostly, stashed away in different bits of the house.

Well, trust him, he was desperate one day and he found the big one, the holiday money. It was more than three hundred pounds in tenners, so it was. I had it rolled up tight and planked in my hair-dryer box in my wardrobe. I don't know, somehow I never imagined Tony going into my hair-dryer – it was a present from him, a really good one. He told me he took the lot because somebody gave him a real dead cert, a horse that couldn't lose, and he just got carried away with this idea that he could come back with thousands in his ears, instead of just hundreds. Well, I came back from the shops and I smelt that he'd been in and I felt quite glad, really, because he'd been so affectionate lately. And then I got this feeling, I don't know how it started, really, I was just putting the kettle on for a cup of coffee. I knew he'd been in and away again and he'd probably pinched a fiver or two and I must admit I was sort of practising a moan, thinking about what I might say to Bella later when I went through to her house for a blether. 'Do you know what I did this morning?' I heard myself saying, then I realized: he never came back in the morning, either for a raid or for making up to me. He liked the house warm and the kids in bed and me in a good mood or through at Bella's.

So I went to the wardrobe and I opened the hair-dryer

box and I just roared and I thought I would die, I roared so much. I fell on the bed and I punched and kicked for a while. Then I took the wedding picture from the wall and smashed it in the fireplace. Then I took one of his good suits out of the wardrobe and I tore it to bits, I held it under my feet and I ripped and ripped like a maniac. Then I went into the living room and took the cosy off the teapot – it was a china teapot, a really dear one – and threw the pot at the matador on the wall and it smashed to pieces and spilled tea all over the mural and all over my white Axminster carpet. Then I just sat in the chair and howled till the children came home at dinner-time.

So that afternoon I went to Bella and I really meant it. 'I've phoned the lawyer,' says I, 'I don't care if he crawls on his hands and knees up that stair and licks my feet and gives me the crown jewels, I'm finished with that man.'

'You're quite right,' says she, 'he's a wrong one and I've always said that.'

'I was taking the kids to Morecambe this year, they liked it that much the last time we were there,' says I.

'Oh, he's just a pig, that man,' says she. 'You should have flung him out years ago, Mina, you're too soft.'

'I know Bella, I'm always saying that myself. Oh, but this time I could really kill him. Just let him try and crawl back. Just let him come with one of those bracelets of his, I'll throw it in his face, so I will.' Then I howled and howled again, I couldn't stop myself, and Bella put her arm around me and gave me a big hug.

Of course Bella told the whole building and everybody was talking about it and saying Tony was in South America. And I must admit there were some that said I'd only got what I deserved, me with my glass doors and my three hundred pound pictures. But most of them said what a terrible life I had with that man and what a terrible thing he'd done to me even although he was such a nice man when he was sober. Then a whole week went and not a whisper from Tony and I was walking about the place feeling like a widow and everybody condoling with me and I think every car that drew up in the road they thought it was the lawyer. Then I did a great big shopping and shut the door and just stayed in for another whole week, I was so fed up with them looking at me like that. But the Wednesday came and I went to Bella's for a cup of tea as usual and that was when I gave the game away and she got such a surprise she nearly died. It was really funny so it was, so I'll tell it like a story.

There I was sipping my tea as usual and we hadn't breathed a word about you-know-who, not a word. Then about half-past four, a bit earlier than usual, up I gets and says, 'Well thanks for the tea, Bella, I better go though and get something ready for Tony's tea, he said he'd be in about six.'

I said it casual, sort of, just for a laugh, just to see her face. Well you can imagine, she nearly died.

'What?'

'Yes,' says I, still casual, 'he came back last night.'

Bella was shocked. It really surprised me the way she spoke, she's not a very nice speaker at the best of times, but she was really terrible.

'I thought you were finished. I thought you'd flung that dirty swine out on his arse for good. I thought that silly effer was in that America or somewhere,' says she.

I told her no, he'd just been in England with his people.

'But he's a wrong one,' says she, 'you were wanting a divorce.'

'Well I know,' says I, 'but you know how it is.'

'Mina, hen,' says she, 'you're making a big mistake. Did he bring back your money?'

'No, no,' says I, 'he's really skint. But he gave me a crocodile.'

That really shocked her, she nearly died.

'A *what*?' says she.

'A crocodile,' says I. 'Come and see it.'

Well, she came through to my house and I took her into the bedroom and led her up to the window-sill.

'Look,' says I.

It's a glass tank with rocks and plants and a little pool in it, I've still got it, and the crocodile just sits there with its legs on a flat rock and its feet sort of dangling in the water. It's only a little thing, about a foot long, sort of dark green with these lovely yellow eyes.

Bella nearly had a heart attack. 'Dear Christ,' says she, 'what's that when it's at home?'

'It's a crocodile,' I told her, 'come and get a look at it.'

Bella's very scared of animals – for her they're all just rats, she doesn't see any differences. She came up to it on tiptoe, not saying a word, and she stared at it for ages.

'Is it alive?' says she.

'Yes,' says I, 'but it doesn't move much. You have to watch for ages then you see it breathing. And once it blinked, it looked really funny.'

'Where the hell did he get it from?'

'Some man in the fair-ground gave him it, at Doncaster.'

'Doncaster.' She looked at it again. 'That sort of thing turns my stomach, rats and things.'

'It's not like a rat,' says I. 'It's really quite nice, you get quite fond of it.'

'Oh Mina,' says she, 'did he really squander all that money, that three hundred pound? I think you should put him in jail.'

'Oh I know I should,' says I, 'he's just a no-user. I could've killed him, so I could. When I heard that wee knock on the door last night I knew right away it was him and I went to the sink and I got a knife, I really did. Then he came in with this thing and he put it down right in the middle of the table. It had a cloth over it.'

I could see Bella shivering when she imagined it sitting on the table. 'What did you say to him?' says she.

'Well, I just lifted the cloth and looked and I nearly dropped dead when I saw the thing lying there.'

'And what did you say?' says Bella.

'Well, I looked at the thing, and I looked at the knife – I still had it in my hand, see – and I looked at Tony.'

'What did you say to him?'

'Well, Bella, I mean, well, what *can* you say to a man that brings you home a crocodile?'

Love and Mongooses

With his unwashed coalman's face and his black clothes and his unfathomable Donegal mumble Big Sean was, to his family as to his neighbours, a largely mysterious thing, fuliginous to the very edge of invisibility. And Michael, his third, was as green as *he* was black.

Sniffer, they called him. His nose was an inexhaustible fountain of green slime. His upper lip was chafed raw by his ceaseless involuntary gesture of sweeping across it with his sleeve or some other part of his rough woollen jersey. He was all slime, and indiscriminately, ubiquitously, he spat it out in chesty green gobs.

Sniffer – he accepted his sobriquet willingly enough, pleased that it distinguished him from the dull legion of Michaels who lived in that and the neighbouring closes, though there were occasions, solemn in their nature, when his real name took on an air of the archangelic which he also found pleasing, and when he insisted upon its use. These occasions always involved dealings with the younger boys, his minions, and the insistence did not have to be shouted, but took the form of a pointed imperious silence, and a refusal to respond to any remark or request in which the proper form was not observed.

Boys two or three years younger than himself, whom he could lead and impress with his fourteen-year-old strength and could tempt into games so silly and so dangerous that his peers would never have countenanced them, were his natural companions. So much did his staying-power surpass theirs, however, that he often found himself alone, absorbed in some repetitive brainless pastime long after they had drifted off to fresh mischief. For his part, he would give up only when threat or accident or hunger compelled him.

Or defeat. One soft summer evening he was posted by the corner traffic lights. The cars, a thin evening straggle of them, would queue at the lights, and he would spit at them, aiming for the nearside front window. Success was a hit on the body of the car, triumph, a firm splat on the glass, total joy, a shot through an open window to the passenger or beyond him to the driver. After his cobra-strike he would turn and disappear into No. 6 close, and through to the trackless waste of backcourts, and no driver had as yet been incensed enough to abandon his vehicle at the head of the queue in order to pursue him. It was a war in which all the advantages lay with the lightly armed guerrilla who struck when least expected and who knew his terrain intimately.

Wee Pete Simpson and John Findlay, at a loose end, joined Sniffer at the corner and offered some supporting fire. Their efforts were half-hearted: for them the sport was in marvelling at the force and accuracy of Sniffer's assaults, and in the mad retreats through the backcourts with the drivers' curses echoing thrillingly through the tiled cavern of No. 6.

On this occasion there was to be the added thrill of an unheard-of thing: a defeat for Sniffer. The enemy for him was an impersonal, unindividualized thing, of interest merely as a target, albeit a dangerous one that might, but probably would not, retaliate. Cooler, Wee Pete and John recognized in the Ford Prefect that turned into the Road from Glenfield Street a victim who had received a damaging hit three minutes before. The driver had swung around the block left into Kenny Street, left into Glenfield Street, left again into the Road.

'Don't tell him,' John whispered to Wee Pete. 'We'll get a laugh.'

As the car drew near, Sniffer loaded his artillery and tensed himself for the rapid head-flick, like Jimmy McGrory heading for goal, that would provide the force. The driver too had plainly geared himself for combat: there was no sedate deceleration to the line, but a mad Chicago-rush and a screeching halt, tyres burning as they brushed the kerb. Sniffer, surprised and bewildered, hesitated and was lost. The driver leaned across to the open nearside window and shot an expert laughing gob hard into his face, then swung into gear again and roared through the changing lights into Tower Street and off through the grey canyons of Springburn.

It was to be a long time before John and Wee Pete had their laugh over this incident: the moment itself was tragic. Sniffer stood in shocked horror, trying to take in what had happened. Then his grief found voice and his troops were hit with the full force of it.

'Aaaaaaahhhh!' He staggered back against the wall between No. 6 and the door of the National Commercial, then slipped down and howled into his dirty knees.

'The bastit! The dirty stinking fucking bastit! Fucking dirty cheater!'

John and Wee Pete knelt one on either side of his heaving shoulders and proffered comfort.

'Never mind Sniffer, that was a pure bastit, that guy,' said Wee Pete.

'Aye,' added John. 'You'd've murdered him in a fair battle, nae bother.'

But Sniffer was not to be consoled. He wiped his face with his sleeve, looked abjectly at the green mingling of his own spit with his enemy's, and howled against the injustice of it all. 'The dirty fucking bastit – look what he done!'

They helped him to his feet, enjoying their rôle now, and escorted him to the first house, first landing, where Big Elsie was ready with limitless motherly warmth.

'It was terrible, Mrs O'Hara,' Wee Pete said. 'A big man just spat on him, right in his face.'

'Oh, if I could get my hauns on him, if Big Sean could get his hauns on the bastit, he'd gie him spit, Christ.'

Sniffer sobbed into her enveloping breast. 'It wasnae fair, Mammy, he never even warned me.'

'Och, never you mind, son, they drivers is just bastits, so they are.'

'It was really terrible, Mrs O'Hara, a big greener, right in his face.'

Wee Pete's reminder brought a new sob of rage and grief; but Sniffer was beginning to enjoy it himself now. His defeat was, in a sense, a victory such as he had never known. His own heroic frontal assaults stood in glorious contrast to the driver's treachery; his huge warm mother loved him; John and Wee Pete, who had come to laugh, had stayed to admire. There was comfort in an honourable defeat, and a sureness that the world knew where the just cause resided.

'I hope he crashes his motor, the big bastit, I wish he crashes it and gets deid,' he said.

'Me tae,' said Wee Pete.

'Me tae,' said John.

'He likely will, son,' said Big Elsie, and they sat silent for a while in a grieving huddle, a fireside pieta, the mother hugging her stricken son, the friends squatting on either side of her chair.

'That driver was a pure cheater,' said John, speaking mostly to himself. 'He never gied Michael a chance, he was like one of they mongooses you see in the pictures, so he was.'

Sniffer sniffed his agreement and gratitude. His confidence in the justicers above was now, like his love, total.

John Findlay, his best pal, had won that love with an apple on a sunny morning in the holidays.

A Saturday it was: he came down into the close with it, into the sweetness of cat's pee and cast-off chip paper and Tam Burke's Friday-night vomit. He was shy of biting into the apple's glossy perfection – wanted in any case to enjoy the anticipatory cringe in his throat at the prospect of the first faint sourness. He jumped over the bottom three steps, avoiding the vomit, and paused to consider whether he should seek his adventures out front in the Road or in the backcourt. Sunshine and morning traffic drew him to the front. He broke the skin of the apple with his two front teeth, preparing to slice a neat strip from the whole circumference by turning it slowly against the edge of his teeth.

At the closemouth he met Sniffer coming in from the Road.

'Hello there, Johnnie boy, what you daein?'

'Nothing much – just hingin aboot.'

'Hey, be a pal, gies a bit of your apple, I'm starving tae death, honest to God I am.'

The generous response came naturally enough: John was not one to keep his things to himself, and he knew that Sniffer was utterly open-handed in his dealings with the world. He handed over the apple and watched while Sniffer plunged his teeth into the scarcely-broached skin, pressing the fruit into his mouth with the full palm of his hand. And watching, he saw the sharp green of the apple, bright against the softer green that oozed around it from the nose and upper lip, and his stomach lurched. Sniffer, having solicited a bite and no more, swallowed his portion and handed the ruined apple back. Seeing the exposed white flesh now streaked with green, John had to fight to keep his stomach down as he spoke:

'Listen, Sniffer, just you keep it – I wasnae hungry, and you're starving tae death.'

Accustomed to making such gestures himself, Sniffer was nevertheless overwhelmed to receive them from others.

'Johnnie boy, you're a pal for life, cross my heart, God strike me doon deid.'

He shuffled off into the fuzzy darkness of the close, and John was left blinking at the sunlight and fighting down the combined assaults of nausea and grief.

The holiday morning was blighted, and there was a painful throbbing knot in his throat as he stepped out into the Road. Nor would the tears be stemmed: as he reached the end of the Ovaltine hoarding that filled the space between the close and No. 14, the pressure became unbearable, and the sluice opened. Guilt at the selfishness of misery served only to worsen it: he cried for the loss of his apple, and he cried because he was crying for the loss of it.

The too patent display of feeling on the Road embarrassed him, and he turned into No. 14, seeking the privacy of the backcourt. And in a mirror-image of their previous encounter, he found himself face to face with Sniffer who had been walking in a parallel course to his own, through the backcourt on the opposite side of the hoarding. The too too visible tears roused Sniffer to ferocious solicitude.

'What's the matter, Johnnie boy? Did somebody hit you?'

He had finished the apple.

'Naw, Sniffer, it's aw right.'

'Come on, tell us who hit you – I'll mollicate the bastit, so I will.'

'Honest, naebody hit me . . . it's just . . . I've got a sore stomach. That's how I gied you the apple, I wisnae feeling like it.'

'Sure? Nae kidding?'

'Nae kidding, honest tae God Sniffer.'

'Just you tell me, Johnnie boy . . . wham bam, send for the cleaners . . . I'll murder the bastit.' His fists were clenched and the battle had already been fought in his head. 'Because you're my best pal, Johnnie boy, you're my best pal a mile.'

John left him and walked through the backcourt to the rear entrance of the close. The glow of Sniffer's declaration was on him, and the sun was shining, and it was holidays, and even nine-year-olds can laugh.

Angels

'You're lovely, so you are, really really lovely. Sometimes I think we've only got you here on loan, you're that lovely.'

She set the brush down on the dressing table and paused to admire the loveliness. It was manifest as much in the cascading golden tresses that she had brushed to an electric sheen as in the pale solemn little face that smiled out of the mirror at her.

'Lovely lovely.'

Mina Sandison's adoration was no mere maternal prattling; it was shared by almost everyone who knew Louise. Drunken men who routinely kicked their wives and threw bottles at buses because the passengers' scarves were the wrong colour would catch their breath and blink at the sight of her; and screeching harridans whose every instinct should have compelled them to denounce her as a simpering spoiled brat smiled and called her a wee angel. Her mother dressed her in angel-white and refused to cut her hair or let her dirty her hands and spoke to her in a special reverentially silly voice, but not even these idiocies could detract from her essential loveliness.

'Lovely lovely.'

She stroked the tresses tenderly with her fingers.

Louise did not play with the other children, but they bore her no grudge.

'Lovely angel. Will you take these things up to your Uncle Michael now? He'll be lonely.'

Louise took up the grapes and the chocolate and laid them in her little white basket.

'Just go straight up to your Uncle Michael's, and don't speak to any big bad wolves on the stairs.'

Louise smiled. She knew her stories well.

Uncle Michael. Michael Connolly, lived two floors above, in the first house on the top landing. He was a fairly distant cousin of Mina's, but she had assumed a proprietorial interest in his well-being because he was sickly and because she hated Margot, his buxom wife. He had TB and a bad stomach and a sheen of nervous sweat on his face. With his bulging eyes and his big nose and his permanent shy stoop, he looked almost deformed beside Louise's ethereal grace; yet there was a bond between them, if only because he, like her, had about him an odour of evanescence.

'My God, darling, you don't look long for this world, you really don't,' Margot had once said, forgetting herself and tripping into honesty. And Michael had believed her.

He read books and thought a lot and was no less a Catholic for being horribly lapsed. Father Coutts was not one of your intellectual Jesuits who relish an argument and sportingly flex their muscles for the fight against free-thinking apostasy. He was the shepherd, his flock was his flock, and there was to be no dialogue with the wolf. If straying lambs could be teased gently back to the fold, fine; but the stakes were too high to allow for pampering. There was no compromising with the Devil in any of his guises – Orangeman or fat whore or, most likely in the case of Michael Connolly, Bertrand Russell.

Michael was the only adult in the tenement who visited the Tower Street library regularly, and his borrowings were no innocent westerns or war-stories or whodunnits, but peril-strewn things from the section by the big window – politics and psychology and theology and philosophy. Not that he showed the slightest outward sign of the corruption that these anti-scriptures must have been working: he attended Mass more frequently than most; he drank with freakish moderation; he gave off no smell of sexual transgression. No – his sins, as his confessions amply revealed, were in the mind and of the mind. It was a mind, however, that grew increasingly tormented, and Father Coutts had resolved to ease its suffering.

The marriage to Margot McCann was, after twelve years, stubbornly childless, but the Father had satisfied himself that there was no impiety in the explanation of this, though neither he nor the couple knew where the fault lay. The oddest of mixes, Margot and Michael lived together in serene harmony. She was a big, strong, curvaceous woman who flaunted her sexuality, outraging the other women with her boldness towards their men, and she openly dominated her ascetic little husband. During their engagement before the War, they had gone rambling in a carefree threesome with Dan Lawson, Margot's cousin and Michael's golf-partner – a man built to the same liberal specifications as Margot herself. He was still a regular caller, and the three were still to be seen together, not hiking on Ben Lomond now, but drinking in the Balmoral Arms. Still more scandalously, Margot and Dan would sometimes leave Michael at home with his books and go off on a pub-crawl together. Between them, the stout wholesome Dan and the frail cerebral Michael seemed to provide for most of Margot's needs. She and Dan were not shy about touching each other in company, but notwithstanding the stair-head gossip, they were both too steeped in their Catholic upbringing and in their shared affection for Michael to admit seriously adulterous aspirations. Margot enjoyed life, and Michael was happy to let her.

It was not *her* sinfulness that tormented him, but his own. Tender to his bootsoles, he found himself progressively unable to acknowledge the vengeful God of Father

Coutts's diatribes. He looked around him and saw sin – but more than that he saw weakness; saw too, that some of the gentlest of his acquaintances were outwith the fold and so of necessity damned.

And for not accepting the certainty of their damnation, he was himself certainly damned. His most fearful imaginings, when his thoughts turned thitherwards, were not of his own flesh eternally roasting, but of his eyes eternally forced to witness the torments of others whom he had loved. He did not reckon, with his bad chest and stomach, that he had many years left beyond the thirty-eight he had already suffered in this world. The need to settle his spiritual affairs, then, pressed heavily upon him.

There was scant comfort to be had from the books. He had come late to reading, found discrimination difficult, and generally aligned his views with whatever authority he was currently discovering. He had variously accepted, with mingled relief and guilt, the Descartian demolition, the Spinozan rapprochement, the Humian pooh-pooh, the Kantian reconstruction, the Nietzschean bombardment – even accepted them all simultaneously, in that each in its way offered a lifeline.

But in his belly he remained an Augustinian: the fire was real, the course had been mapped out at zero-hour, and he was almost certainly damned. He had been off work for the last two weeks because of his chest, and while Margot was out at her job in the telephone exchange, he had had a lot of time to brood upon death, and upon his own depravity, and to translate his vague dread of the flames into a terrifying certitude. And although he horrified himself even as he formulated his thoughts, he grew slowly to believe that, faced with the cold inexorability of damnation, his only clear course was this: to deserve it utterly. An eternity of brooding upon how narrowly he had missed salvation itself seemed unacceptable.

A small incident from his childhood recurred constantly to his mind, and unwrote Kant. The toffee factory had closed down, or shifted its operation to some other part of the city, and the abandoned building had become the object of nightly forays by the tenement boys, who competed with one another in throwing stones through the windows. Eventually the authorities lost patience, and enlisted the power of the Church against the malefactors. Father Reilly had come to the school and addressed them at morning assembly, warning them thoroughly of the fiery consequences of sin. And the same night, as the gang assembled for another vandalistic excursion, he, Michael, had assumed the spokesman's rôle for the Catholics in their en masse refusal to take part.

'It's OK for yous,' he said to the mocking Protestants, 'but we go tae Hell for breaking windaes. Father Reilly told us this morning.'

'Aye, and we go forever,' said Timothy McCann, lending support to the argument.

The Protestants were indignant. 'Huh', snorted Willie Jackson, 'think you're smart, eh? Well we go tae Hell for breaking windaes as well, so there!'

Michael was almost thrown by this, not because he did not know the answer to it, but because it pained him to deliver it. 'But . . . but . . . yous are going to Hell anyway.'

The theological dispute followed, and even as he warmed to it and enjoyed it, he felt the pain of knowing it was only a game, that however much they might feel there was something to be said on their side, his friends from the other school were utterly and God-ordainedly wrong. As he argued mock-angrily that they were for the eternal fire, so he knew, sadly, that the argument could alter nothing, was mere noise. Alec and Willie and David and all the rest – his friends – were damned. The images that the thought had planted in his mind, drawn from Father Reilly's dire sermon, had taken firm root, and returned nightly to haunt his dreams.

He wished, then, neither to be saved nor to be almost-saved: all that was left was to ensure that he should not spend eternity grieving for the harshness of his sentence.

He planned to strangle his niece Louise, the loveliest thing in his immediate world, with the lace of his old rambling-boot, when she made her morning visit. He would strangle her, then strip her and mutilate her face. Then he would leave her naked on his fireside carpet, go down to the second storey to ask Mina if he could use her telephone, and call the police. He would not kill himself, because that might cause some small stirrings of pity. He would face the incredulous horror of the family, the tenement, the world, then he would be hanged, and there would be no wrangling over his soul. He knew he was capable of the strangling, but wondered at the final act, the mutilation. And yet he must steel himself for it, because it was required, he felt, for the circumvention of Christ's mercy, which might be infinite. Total forgiveness could only be met by total depravity.

It was half-past ten; she usually arrived about eleven, so there was time for his preparations. He drew the lace out of his boot and put it in his trouser pocket, then he set up the draughtboard.

He had taught her the game some weeks before, and took delight in playing with her because her approach to it seemed to shadow-forth the total goodness of spirit that, given the idiocy of the mother and the profligacy of the father, could only have come direct from God. Her quick little brain had absorbed the rules almost instantly, and she could, if she had been so minded, have beaten him or at least played him down to a draw on most occasions. But the idea of the game as a contest did not engage her at all:

she invested the board, the pieces, the individual squares even, with a personality, and used the tedious rules of draughts as a means of playing out her own small romances. She would move a piece into instant death because it looked tired and might want to come off for a little rest, and would use it later to crown a forager to the back row – but only if it looked sufficiently rested. When he removed her last piece, as he invariably did, she would see it simply as the signal to set the board up again, and to exchange colours – there was no defeat, and no victory.

He arranged the board with the white pieces for her, and placed a glass of milk at her side of the table. And fingering the lace in his pocket, he waited.

He sweated harder when he heard her firm small knock at the door, and his chest tightened painfully. Opening the door, he was freshly astonished at her loveliness. He would, on a normal morning, have patted her head, taken her avuncularly by the shoulder, but his hands refused.

'Hello, Uncle Michael. Are you feeling better now? These are from Mummy.'

He took the gifts, mumbling his thanks.

'Come in, pet, I've poured a wee drop of milk, come on in.'

She sat at the draughtboard, sipped the milk.

'I've not been to school this week, Mummy kept me home, she thought I had a headache. We've been reading books.'

'Oh, that's nice, sweetheart. Is your headache better now?'

'Yes, it was only Mummy. We read *The Secret Garden*. Have you read that, Uncle Michael?'

He wished he had.

'It's really sad at first, but there's a garden that makes everybody nice again, a sort of magic garden, but it's not really magic, just a lovely garden. I think I'll make the draughts a magic garden this time.'

And she did. And he was mesmerized again by her natural beauty and grace which his bootlace was about to extinguish.

There was a solemn thought-furrow on her white brow as she considered her move. Perhaps, he thought, Mina isn't such a fool, with her silly voice and her white dresses and her keeping the child apart. Perhaps she knows for sure something the rest of us just feel. There was a book lying on the table, open and face downwards. Father Coutts had lent him it in the hope that time spent with this might allow less for more dangerous things: *The Revelation to the Monk of Evesham*. He picked it up and read at the place he had left off the night before:

> For ther ys no synne wretyn in holy scripture
> but ther ys ordende in the placys certen peynis to
> al that be doers of hem!

'There.' She pushed a white piece into the centre where it might speak again to its friend who had abandoned it at the beginning of the game. 'They'll be happier now.'

He drew his fingers across his brow and smelt on them the hair-oil that had seeped down with the sweat from his scalp.

'Your move, Uncle Michael.'

Your move.

He reached his left hand across the table as his right drew the lace from his pocket. He touched her chin gently with the backs of his fingers. Under the table, his legs felt damp. A lump of phlegm in his chest seemed to be pushing against his ribs, choking him.

She smiled, then a frown of concern puckered her face.

'Are you all right, Uncle Michael? You look very hot.'

The effort of trying to speak brought on the cough. It came with sudden frightening force after two short heaving gasps, and his hand, reaching for his mouth, was not quick enough to prevent a small fine spatter of blood from hitting her breast. Hardly a fairy's thimbleful, it looked ghastly against the pristine whiteness of her dress.

The panic was all his. Louise moved round to his side of the table and put her hand on his shoulder.

'You're not well again, Uncle Michael – I'll go and tell my Mummy to phone for the doctor.'

'No, I'm OK sweetheart – your lovely dress.'

'I've got fifteen dresses. Sometimes I get nose-bleeds and its much worse than that. You come with me and Mummy can phone the ambulance then phone Auntie Margot and tell her you've gone in for a rest and you're all right really.'

They went downstairs together, the child leading the man by the hand. Mina's soft spot for her cousin cancelled her shock at the sight of her angel all blood-flecked, and brought out the woman of affairs, who knew the use of telephones and could look doctors in the eye.

They took Michael into the infirmary for tests, and Mina soaked Louise's dress in Rinso.

Telling the story to Bella Findlay that evening, she was all family warmth:

'That Michael's just an angel, so he is. There he is coughing up blood, and the only thing he's worried about is my wee Louise's dress. Imagine that – she's got hundreds of dresses and she's really too big for that one, she's nearly nine now. Him nearly dying, poor soul, and all he can think about is the wean's dress. Right enough, it did look terrible, that blood, I got quite a fright myself, and I'm not easy frightened. But him – the wean's dress, her lovely white dress, that's all he could say. He's an angel, Bella, sure as I'm standing here, a pure angel. That Margot McCann doesn't know how lucky she is, silly bitch.'

And Bella, since he was her favourite cousin too, agreed.

The Fall of Bumpstead Ruskin

Sandra was no Willie Shakespeare – she knew that and Mr Blair knew it – but she wrote shorthand with some aplomb and the fair copy was clear and the spelling reasonable and as long as she got the official forms filled in Mr Blair didn't care a bean how much or how little she accomplished for the Slum Clearance Survey; that wasn't his department. For her part, she looked to the official forms, which the tenants had either filled in already or would fill in with her help when she visited, as a useful toe in the door for the much thicker, much richer, but non-obligatory Slum Clearance Questionnaire. She could appear as The Woman From The Corporation then, not as a mere researcher from the college, and her questions could take on an official status that might promote respect and, with it perhaps, eloquence.

She had rehearsed her approach often enough in her head: 'Hello, I'm from the Housing Department – I've come to enquire whether you need any assistance with your rehousing form.'

They always would, of course, and once admitted to the living-room, she could slip in the main business: 'Now there's another thing, Mr and Mrs Thingammy. As you may know, the Corporation is launching a major slum clearance scheme – your rehousing is part of it – and they require information from as many people as possible. It will be treated in the strictest confidence, of course.'

She imagined, foolishly, that she would be able to wrap the whole thing up in four preliminary visits, one day for each landing, plus a single day, a week or two later, for t-crossing and i-dotting.

She arrived, then, on a Monday morning to do the first landing, flipped her mental coin and decided she would begin at the house furthest from the staircase and work in reverse order along the landing to the O'Haras in the first house.

Things began to go awry before her knuckles even touched the fourth door. During the moment when she stood poised for knocking and mustering her thoughts for her first interview, the door abruptly swung open and she saw an urgent greasy head bent threateningly towards her at breast height. It tilted upwards, paused for three seconds while the eyes took her in, then bent again as the man brushed past her to rush along the landing and down the stairs to the close. The door stayed awkwardly open and she found herself staring with some embarrassment into a tight little lobby with floral wallpaper and a brass plaque showing two windmills and a row of clogged Dutch-girls. She was desperately considering her next move when a woman stepped out from the living-room with the evident intention of pushing the door closed. The woman was startled at the sight of a stranger on the doorstep, and her voice was suspicious and nervously hostile.

'Do you want something?'

'Hello, eh . . . Mrs Ruskin? I'm from the Corporation – it's about your rehousing form.'

'Oh my God, we havenae done that yet – is that bad? You'll have to speak to my man, so you will.'

Sandra smiled and made her reassuring noises and was reluctantly shown into the living-room where she invited Jessie Ruskin to spread the rehousing form on the table, and took a pen from her brief-case for the filling-in.

They moved without hitch through the matter-of-fact opening sections: names and ages of occupants; number in full employment; weekly rent; recent repairs; current problems. Hesitation first came, as she had expected, at Box 10: Rehousing Requirements – favoured areas, in rank order from first to third.

'You'll need to wait for my man for that one – I cannae dae that one myself cause him and me don't really see eye tae eye on it.'

'Was that your husband I . . . met at the door?'

'Aye, that's him away for his *Daily Record* and his run round the block – he'll be back any minute now.'

'Oh that's lovely. And what exactly is it you don't agree about, Mrs Ruskin?'

'Ach, it's just I'm fed up with the toon. I'd like a nice new hoose, in a scheme, like, with a bathroom and hot and cold watter and maybe even a wee gerden if it's a low-doon hoose. Know what I mean? But Bumpstead, he likes the toon. He'd like to stay here even if it's another old building, and another old hoose like this.'

'Bumpstead?'

'Aye, he likes it here. That's him back.'

Urgent footsteps were followed by the slamming of a door, and the greasy head came in.

Bumpstead Ruskin was shocked and displeased to find a stranger at his table, and his thoughts turned precipitately to his dole money, to spies.

'You fae the broo?' he asked aggressively.

His wife stepped in to defuse the situation. 'Naw, Bumpstead, this is The Woman Fae The Corporation, about they whityecallit things, they forms for a new hoose – she's been helping me to write it, so she has.'

In her voice, in her very stance towards her man, there was something touching on fear.

'Oh, that's aw right then.' He sat down, and they completed the official form, entering Castlemilk and Local as first-equal choices in Box 10.

Box 15, the last box, invited tenants to state special requirements arising from disabilities, employment, family responsibilities, etc., and here Bumpstead, who had decided Sandra was an ally and who was beginning to enjoy the nearness of a young, tailored, and faintly perfumed woman, considered for a while, and, in a voice which Sandra could not read, could not identify as serious or frivolous, straightforward or ironic, said:

'Well, I need good blocks to run roon.'

In the only perceptible change she had permitted to take place so far in her expression of timid discontent, Jessie Ruskin frowned.

'Och, Bumpstead, you're aye on about they blocks, gie they blocks a rest, will you?'

'I'm sorry, what sort of blocks do you mean, Mr Ruskin?' Sandra was nonplussed, but she recognized that he was serious.

'It's just that I get these feelings. Every now and again this feeling comes . . . I have tae get up and run roon the block a few times, sometimes one direction, sometimes the other – depends on the feeling. I've got tae dae it, you know, I get this sort of feeling, as if I'm gonnae burst, know what I mean?'

Sandra did not know, but she had wit enough to see her chance.

'Oh, now that's very interesting, Mr Ruskin, that about feelings, because I've got another form here, from the Corporation, and it's about, well, things like that. The Corporation would like to know how people feel about living in these old town tenements. They want to know what it's like for families, what their feelings are like.'

'Feelings?' said Bumpstead Ruskin, straightening up in his chair. 'Don't talk to me about feelings, I get them aw the time, don't I, Jessie?'

'Oh aye, he gets awful feelings,' his wife said, nodding.

'Could you just wait a minute, Mr Ruskin?'

Sandra reached into her brief-case and brought out a Slum Clearance Survey form. 'Now, would you say that you and your wife suffered from lack of space, with two children in this flat?'

Bumpstead closed his eyes and held them closed for a theatrical five seconds before he spoke.

'Space? Space? Don't talk to this boy about space, hen. See space, I'll tell you about space.'

And he told her. And she took it down in shorthand, translating as she wrote, and it was lunchtime when she finished, time for her to be back at the office.

In the afternoon she did not return to the tenement, but sat at a vacant desk and fair-copied her notes. Then she left them on Mr Blair's desk with a memorandum: 'Dear Mr Blair, I'm afraid I only got one form back today, I'll get more tomorrow. My very first tenant kept me all morning and I thought you might be interested in what he said and might want to read it before I pass it up to Slum Clearance, Sandra.'

Mr Blair, confronted by several pages of neat close script, was less than enthusiastic, but he had finished the *Herald* crossword, and had some time on his hands. So he read, skipping the prefatory remarks about Mr R. H. Ruskin and his family and getting quickly to the transcript of Bumpstead's statement.

A Maryhill man himself, and neither ashamed of nor secretive about his unexalted origins, he had no great difficulty in hearing in his head what Bumpstead had actually said behind Sandra's genteel rendition, and he paid silent tribute, as he read, to her skill as a translator.

> People keep getting in the road, don't they? I mean, you're trying to get somewhere. I just hit them sometimes. They say round here I don't look where I'm

going, that's why they call me Bumpstead, after some guy in the pictures, but that's daft, it's them as gets in the road, I mean I don't bump into lampposts or bus-stops or walls, do I? So that proves it – it's them that don't look, they never see you coming, they just stand in the close or in the shop doors, just when you're wanting past, needing your papers. And they call the wife Soorpuss, that's not right, is it? That old Mrs Sloag – half the time I open the door she's standing there, I think she lives on my doorstep, nosey old bitch. I've hit her a few times. I like it here, but. Except for the lavatories, the lavatories are terrible. It's fine and handy for the shops, so it is. I go out for my paper in the morning, have my pint in the afternoon. I don't go out much at night. I do a lot of handywork for the neighbours, like. They're all putting in these interior grates just now and I do the firebrick for them – I know a guy gets it cheap. I do the cement work, gets me a few bob for my pint, know what I mean?

It's OK up here. There's some right nutters, mind, don't get me wrong, there's some right bammers: that Auld McKinnon up the stair, him that lived in that tent ever since his wife died – twenty-five year or something. That is a real nutter. No wonder they've locked him up. And that whole crowd up on the top flat, that Jessie Brass and her daft daughter and her fancyman, he's a real bampot, he paints his head with bootpolish so's you won't know he's baldy. Christ knows where she dug him up – he must be about seventy, as well, and she's a good-looking woman still, don't get me wrong, she's a good-looking woman. Christ, her man was bad enough, but that headcase!

Me and the wife don't take much to do with the neighbours, we keep ourselves to ourselves, like. That party they had for the Coronation, we never went to that, couldn't be bothered. I just like my paper and my pint and my run round the block. They say I should be in that Olympics, I run that fast. Sometimes I go left at the close and round Tower Street way and sometimes I go right and round Glenfield Street, maybe three or four times.

I just get this feeling, you know? I have to get up and run. Ever since I was a boy. I could never sit still and I used to drop things and trip over things and bump into people – they don't call me Bumpstead for nothing (laugh).

They've reported me to the police up here, so they have. Aye, that Limpy McGlaughlin comes up here one night – big chap on the door, you could tell right away it was the police.

'Sorry to disturb you, Mr Ruskin, but we've received complaints about you,' says he. 'About your behaviour, like.'

'My behaviour?' says I. 'My behaviour? What the hell is that supposed to bloody mean?' I wasn't scared of him, I went to school with his brother, so I did.

'It seems you've been knocking down children and elderly people on the stair,' says he, 'and if it doesn't stop there might have to be charges.'

'Charges?' says I. 'Well you can tell them, son, if they charge me, I'll charge them right back, so there. Anyway, who's been shopping me to you people?'

'I'm not at liberty to say that at the moment,' says he. 'This is only a warning.'

'Don't you give me your bloody warnings, this is a free country, I've got my rights same as anybody else,' says I, and he goes away. That showed him, so it did. These police, they think they can get away with murder, so they do.

I'd like to get away from this mob here. I like the

town, I don't really fancy these schemes, stuck out in the middle of nowhere, but I'd like to go somewhere else, they're a lot of moaning-faces here, I can't stick them.

Mr Blair laid the document down, bored and amused and formulating his mild avuncular rebuke to Sandra. There were still seven pages of her neat script, which he had no intention of reading.

Bumpstead Ruskin lusted after Big Jessie Brass. He ached in every sinew for her fat motherly warmth, though he had never once looked her in the eye. He hated Alan Brass, her profligate and now disappeared husband, and he hated still more The Man With The Painted Heid, her current lover. His dream was of Jessie folding him in her arms, squeezing him till his ribs creaked, carrying him away from Soorpuss, his frightened skinny wife, and his two whimpering children, settling him into her great lap, and hugging him to death between her breasts. In the meantime, separated from her by three storeys, by The Man With The Painted Heid, by his family and by his terror, he ran, crashing into children and old women and kicking dogs and tripping over cats.

To Granny Sloag, the withered crone next door, he was a perpetual real danger. She opened her door timorously, fearful of being smashed to the landing, and she had enlisted the support of other tenants to the extent that several of the men had offered to break his neck and most families had sworn to boycott his handyman services. Few, though, threatened him to his face, because few ever found themselves face to face with him. Even in the pub, when he called in for his nightly pint, he seldom sat down, seldom spoke, except to the barman. Occasionally, when Big Jessie was there, drinking stout in her corner of the lounge with The Man With The Painted Heid licking her neck, he would stay longer, and drink more, and seethe.

His wife had been Jessie McLure, then Jessie Ruskin for the first year of their married life, and thereafter Soorpuss – a blighted woman lacking the wherewithal either to resist her man's domination or to succumb to it happily. She had allied herself with him and shared his unpopularity until, grown weary with the struggle, she saw nothing left but a retreat into sullen silence. Most of the tenants had known her from her youth as a slim healthy smiling girl, one of the six famously attractive daughters of Jock and Belle McLure; a girl who could have her pick and who surrendered too hastily to the meretricious charms of Ronald Ruskin, chancer.

Their house, the fourth on the first landing, was padded and warm, but the air within bristled with discontent and lovelessness.

Bumpstead, in a well-advertised moment of folly, had declared himself to Jessie Brass in the close, presenting his greasy scalp to her face and telling her straight to her feet that she needed a man to share her bed, a man like him. Jessie, who had once or twice in drunken Hogmanay generosity allowed him to fondle her bottom, rebuffed him raucously, laughing in his face and saying she hadn't got rid of one headache only to land herself with another, and she and young Jessica could manage fine by themselves.

Jessie, proud and alone, he could accommodate in his scheme, dissipating his yearnings in headlong tumbles to the papershop and around the block. But when The Man With The Painted Heid assumed the position of Jessie's live-in lover, jealousy tore him like an army of desert ants, and his careering grew wilder by the day. As well as running around the block, he took to running up and down the four flights of the tenement staircase – five, six, seven times at a stretch, reducing himself to a state of collapse and enraging the neighbours as he stumbled against their walls or thumped past their doors.

That he had not long since been beaten into order was testimony to the fact that most of the able-bodied men – such as Big Sean O'Hara and Phil Findlay and Wullie Moore – worked grindingly long hours, and were rarely abroad in the tenement during his daytime or small-hours running. His victims were, in the main, the old women and the children and the feckless men who were as cracked as himself and hardly capable of engaging him in open conflict.

His downfall, when it finally came, followed hard upon a week of ferocious crashing and banging brought on by a session in the pub when The Man With The Painted Heid, egged on by his cronies, was hinting long and loud about his life with Jessie, about her fearsome insatiability and his own glorious exhaustion.

'Aye,' he was saying, 'I thought I was finished, past it – a man my age, like. But Christ, that Big Jessie!'

That Big Jessie. That Big Jessie. It was not the first time Bumpstead had suffered thus in the pub, but it was the worst. The image of her fat white thighs splayed to receive The Man With The Painted Heid, of his knobbly hands clasped upon her wonderful rump, of his loathsome skinniness crushed against her breast, of his white pumping arse – the richness of all that set against the bleakness of his own marital bed was too much, and he charged roaring through the swing-doors and into the Road, running head down towards the Tower Street traffic lights. Eleven times he circled the block, counter-clockwise, before charging upstairs to his own house and falling gasping and sobbing to the carpet in front of the fire.

'What's the matter with you the night?' Soorpuss asked – not expecting, not desiring and not receiving an answer.

She was relieved, after suffering three hours of his sweating and writhing, when she felt him leave the bed in the middle of the night to pound the staircase. Then, night after night he pounded, ruining the sleep of almost everyone in the tenement, making Granny Sloag a terrified prisoner in her own house, waking babies, shattering dreams, until the hitherto unaffected men began to be drawn in, and the threat, 'If he does that waance mair I'll kill him, the daft bastit,' was accurately attributed to more than one of them. Big Elsie O'Hara, panicking when Big Sean was setting off to kill him, had to hang her great bulk around his neck and plead with him not to get himself hanged for a bampot, and Phil Findlay, no issuer of idle threats, announced that Bumpstead's next assault on the floorboards of the second landing would be his last.

Soorpuss was generously exempted from the growing hostility towards the Ruskin household, in recognition of the fact that she suffered more than any of them, and on the first landing there were even stirrings of old, long-lost sympathies:

'She's a poor soul,' Big Elsie said.

'Aye, and she's a lot to put up with, living with that headcase,' Jane Simpson put in.

'I've nothing against her, nothing personal, like,' said old Sloag.

But Soorpuss she was, and Soorpuss she remained, spurning the proffered sympathy, and never wavering in her public support of her man. Each of the other three women had made an overture, hinted at cups of tea, biscuits, a fireside blether; but if their kindness softened something inside, still the ingrained sourness remained to dictate her frowns, her curt refusals.

The poundings continued, and the threats multiplied. And then, at two o'clock on a damp Thursday morning, he fell.

Two hours of tormented writhings had ended when he leapt from the bed and started for his clothes. Soorpuss listened to the familiar sounds as he pulled his trousers over his pyjamas and stepped into his shoes, then wound himself up for his rush to the door by pounding his fists a hundred times on the wall.

Their door was set a yard back from the landing, with the outside door of Granny Sloag's house on the right side of the recess and the stair wall on the left. He saw the stick as he charged out into the landing, and in the steady blue gaslight he took in, while he flew headlong towards the wall opposite, all the details: a piece of oak dowelling, four-and-a-half feet long, was jammed at one end into the crumbling plaster at the point where the skirting met old Sloag's doorpost, and at the other, at precisely the same height, into a hole especially gouged in the wall just above the skirting. Before his head met the opposite wall he knew the whole story and he cursed them, his enemies, and cried out his love for Jessie Brass.

A straight nine inches through that wall Jock Simpson was disturbed in his snoring sleep by the dull violence of the impact.

'You aw right, Jane?' he said. 'You aw right?'

'Shut up and go to sleep,' said Jane.

Bumpstead nearly died. He lay comatose in the infirmary and the doctors said it was touch and go, he might pull through and he might not and even if he did there could be permanent brain damage.

Soorpuss kindled her morning fire with the stick, and it became a legend.

When Sandra made her follow-up visit to the Ruskins, two weeks after her first, she was met at the door by Soorpuss. She had heard about the accident and was eager to offer her condolences. She saw Bumpstead sitting snugly in his armchair by the fire, with his slippered feet perched on the edge of the range: he was reading a book, a Zane Grey western. Responding to her greeting, he smiled up at her, a welcoming and comforting smile.

'They've let him out, just to see,' said Soorpuss, 'but he might have to go back in, it just depends.'

'I won't keep you long,' Sandra said. 'There are just one or two things I'd like to ask you about.'

'Would you like a cup of tea, hen?' Soorpuss asked.

'Well, if it's not too much trouble, Mrs Ruskin.'

'Jessie, hen – my name's Jessie – sit down and rest your weary legs,' said Soorpuss, smiling.

The Three Brass Budgies

There were plenty of folk This Side and even one or two That Side who thought Marciano should have been disqualified against Cockell. Fat Alan Brass, with a fiver on Our Don at twelve-to-one, felt so strongly about it he told Barney the Book that any bookie who didn't return stakes on the fight wasn't British at all but a fucking Yankee-Nazi crook. That kind of talk was completely out of order, even though he was half-canned, and all the other punters on the third landing nodded when Barney told him he could take his custom elsewhere in future. Fat Alan kicked a lot of plaster from the walls and called them all a bunch of Yankee-Nazi bastards and stomped up to the fourth landing to batter young Jessica.

Big Jessie was out at her three-night-a-week cleaning job at the billiard hall. He found young Jessica sitting in the armchair with Tiger the cat on her lap. He grabbed her thick black hair in his left hand and told her she knew fucking well she wasn't supposed to let that cat in the house and it was her fucking fault he had to throw his hard-earned money (he did casual work on building sites) at crooked bastards like Barney the Book. Then he started hitting her about the face with his right hand, and the cat jumped from her lap and clung to the curtain.

'See what I mean?' he said. 'See what I fucking mean? Look at it tearing the curtains.'

Jessica pulled herself free while he was thinking about switching his attack to the cat. Hardly less agile than Tiger, her best and only friend, she slipped easily through the elephantine lunges and, barefoot as she was ran out into the fourth landing and downstairs to the Road, heading for the billiard hall. Tiger curled up under the bed for a while, but finally grew irritated by Fat Alan's unabated rage and padded off into the cool night.

Jessica reached the billiard hall as Big Jessie was putting away her bucket and mop. Big Jessie clenched her fists with anger when she saw the welts on Jessica's face.

'Has that pig been hitting you again, hen?'

'Aye, Mammy, and he hit the cat as well, so he did. He's lost money on that boxing again.'

'Oh has he, well? Well I'll boxing him, I'll money him. That's him finished – that's him oot the bloody door. I've told him repeatedly if he hit you again he was oot on his stupit erse.'

'You gonnae hit him, Mammy?'

'Hit him? Hit him? Hen, I'm gonnae murder the fat bastit.'

When they got back to the house he was gone, and when he returned two days later, ready to be sheepish or aggressive as the moment required, they were playing pontoon for matchsticks and hardly noticed him.

Fat Alan Brass blamed everybody for everything. He wasn't so much fat as paunchy, but a foul-tempered no-user for all that. And young Alan, at eighteen, was out of the same mould. Nobody, least of all Big Jessie and young Jessica, had wiped any cheeks when the son went off to the army, and Big Jessie made no secret of the fact that she'd be reaching for the champagne when the father finally carried out his threat of going to live for good with some or other of his fancy-women.

'We'd get on just lovely – me and the wean and wee Rocky.'

Rocky, brought home one night in a battered cage as a peace-offering, was an amiable blue budgie who spent most of the daylight hours perched on the clothes-pulley proclaiming that Benny Lynch was still king, but who at night, if Tiger wasn't visiting, loved to run about the floor trying to recite the list of heavyweight champions from John L. Sullivan to his own namesake, the newly-desanctified Rocky Marciano. He had been Fat Alan's Wee Champion for a while, but his failure to take the heavyweight list beyond Jim Corbett, John L.'s successor, had led to a cooling of the friendship, and he now aligned himself quite positively with the female half of the family. Bitterly aware of this, Fat Alan nevertheless kept for himself the duty of cleaning out the cage, which he performed with religious regularity and scientific thoroughness every Sunday evening.

And it was on a Sunday evening that the crisis occurred that led to his final unlamented disappearance. Rocky was on the table admiring himself in his mirror, which Jessica had propped up against a cup. Fat Alan had taken the cage to the sink in order to scrub it out. It had been many years since Fat Alan had seen his own feet while standing on them; with a birdcage balanced on his ten-pint paunch, he had no chance. He turned from the sink and at the same instant Rocky, tired of pecking at his reflection, fluttered down to the floor. They met before the bird could even begin his recital. He did not receive Fat Alan's full thirteen stone because Fat Alan felt him through the thin sole of his slipper and drew back – but it was an uneven contest. All three of them stared for a moment in horror at the writhing bundle of blue on the linoleum, then Jessica picked it up.

'His wee heart's still beating,' she said. 'It's like a wee train, so it is.'

But the neck was clearly broken, and within a minute or two the gallant thumps had faltered, gathered pace, faltered again, then stopped.

Fat Alan felt them staring at him – his wife, his daughter and the hovering vengeful soul of the dead budgie, and his face grew red and tears welled up in his eyes as he wound himself up for the offensive.

'My burd! My poor wee burd! That was yous bitches, training him tae walk on the fucking flerr!'

'Training him?' said Big Jessie in her scornful here-we-go-again tone. 'Training him? What the bloody hell you on aboot? You're the only one that's trained him. You and that stupit boxing, that John L. stupit Sullivan. We never trained him nothing, it was you.'

'Aye, and he only learned two of them anyway,' said Jessica, who was beginning to cry, but was enjoying her father's guilt.

'We never trained him nothing,' Big Jessie repeated.

'Yous did sot! Yous did! Yous should've learnt the wee bastit tae stay up high like a real burd, for Christ's sake. Burds are no supposed tae run aboot the fucking flerr.'

'Och, shut up, you big stumor. Naebody learnt him that – he learnt that hissel.'

While they argued, young Jessica smoothed the feathers of the corpse. There was a pause while Fat Alan fished around for other culprits, other offences, and she looked up.

'We'll need tae bury him – wi a wee cross, maybe. You've killt him, Da.'

This, the direct accusation, was too much for Fat Alan.

'Jesus Christ, what've I just been saying? It wasnae me that killt the wee bastit, it was yous. What would I want tae kill him for? He's my Wee Champion, Christ – I've been teaching him tae speak.'

'I don't believe this – I really don't.' Big Jessie was pointing at the floor, where a few small feathers stood out clean and blue against the faded brown linoleum. 'We've just seen you stauning on the wee bugger, haven't we?'

'That's immaterial, immaterial – yous were the cause of it.'

'Och,' she said, shaking her head. 'Don't listen tae him, Jessica, hen, he's just a heidcase, he's pure mental. Come on we'll bury the wee thing doon the back.'

'Hey, haud your fucking horses,' Fat Alan interrupted, 'he's my burd – it's me that buries him. And who do you think you're calling mental?'

'Who do I think? Well I only see one bampot aroon here, and it's no me, and it's no the wean, and it's no that wee burd, so there.'

He considered punching, considered slapping, considered strangling; but Big Jessie was a match for him, and there was blood on his slipper.

'Wait till I tell our Alan aboot this,' he said lamely.

'Shut your face,' said Big Jessie, knowing she had the ascendancy, and that nothing more elaborate was required.

'He'll have something tae say aboot this, just you wait.'

'He'll say the same as everybody else – that you're a bloody nutter.'

'I want that burd. Gie me that burd, you.'

Jessica looked towards her mother, and her fingers tightened.

'Don't gie him it, hen, you and me'll bury it doon the back.'

'I want that burd!'

'Away 'n' bile your heid.'

'I want that fucking burd!'

'Well you're no fucking getting it, so there.'

He lunged at Jessica's hand, but both women were too quick for him. Jessica retreated to the door, and Big Jessie planted herself in front of him, blocking his way. He tried another lunge and they were wrestling, Jessie strong with righteousness and him half-hearted at first with guilt, but growing more violent as his frustration mounted.

Knowing he would ultimately prove too strong for her, Big Jessie simplified the funeral arrangements; whatever happened, he would not get his hands on the bird.

'Jessica,' she shouted, 'go and put it down the lavvy – hurry up, hen.'

He roared his rage and his fat face reddened as he tried to prise loose her grip.

'Come back here wi that burd,' he screamed as Jessica ran through the door and into the landing.

The lavatory was four steps across the lobby. He put his leg behind Big Jessie's and tripped her and they fell together to the floor. He ripped himself free and was beginning his rush for the door when the sound of the flushing toilet stopped him short.

Big Jessie was frightened now, doubting her ability to hold him long enough for young Jessica to find sanctuary in one of the other houses if he chose to vent his rage on her. But the rage had given way to grieving self-pity. He sat on the floor and howled.

'My fucking burd! My wee Rocky – doon the fucking closet. It's no fair!'

Ready enough for reconciliation, she put on the rough cajoling tone that was the nearest she ever came to tenderness in her dealings with him.

'Shut up and I'll make us a cup of tea.'

'Fuck your tea,' he said, rebuffing her.

'That's right – blame me, blame the wean, blame every bugger but yoursel. Och – your heid's full of broken bottles.'

'Don't you talk tae me like that.'

'Well don't you be so stupit then.'

'Cause listen: I don't have to take that fae you or anybody else, right? One word merr fae you and I'd be oot that door.'

'What?'

'You heard me. There's plenty places where I'd be welcome, don't you worry.'

Big Jessie was suddenly excited: she saw the winning move, but was enjoying the game too much to make it immediately.

'What, wi a face like that?' she said.

'Ha, ha, never you mind my face, there's plenty don't think it's so bad. One word fae you and I'll be oot that door like a shot.'

She could hold it back no longer: she waited just long enough for the silence to settle, then, in a quiet voice, said:

'Word.'

He half-understood, but had to be sure.

'What?'

'One word, you said, one merr word. Well there it is – word word word word word.'

'Right – if that's the way you want it.'

'Never mind the speeches, we don't need speeches, just get the fuck oot and leave me and the wean in peace.'

And he was gone in the time it took him to change into outdoor shoes and put on his jacket.

Big Jessie went across to the lavatory and knocked gently on the door.

'Jessica, you in there, hen?'

'Aye Mammy.'

'Come on oot, hen, it's aw right, your da's away.'

Young Jessica opened the door.

'There's still feathers floating in the pan, Mammy. I've pulled the plug aboot a hunner times, so I have.'

'Never you mind, hen,' said Big Jessie, putting a comforting arm around her shoulder. 'We'll get another wee burd, and we'll call it Rocky as well.'

And they did.

Rocky II was blue like Rocky I, and gentle, but he never

learned to talk, beyond an incorrigibly bird-like attempt at 'Cuppa tea for Rocky'.

With Fat Alan gone, young Jessica was neglected by her mother as much as she had ever been, but it was a happy loving neglect, and she relished her nights alone in the house now that she was freed from the constant fear that he would come home to blame her face for all the ills of the universe. Slap-happily, Big Jessie made no objection to Tiger spending the colder nights curled on her sofa; he kept the mice down, and as long as Rocky was safe in his cage there were no obvious dangers. He was a clean cat, and good company for Jessica.

Young Jessica blossomed. She took to having some of the other children round of an evening, not often enough to cheapen the experience for them or for herself, but occasionally, when the wind told her the time was right. She turned off the gas mantle and lit candles and built up a great fire and told them stories about The Man With The White Sandshoes.

Although she had lived all of her fourteen years in the tenement, the fact that she attended neither the Protestant nor the Catholic, but the Special School for mental deficients, gave her an edge of foreignness. In a single year she had stretched from a plumpish thing into a stringy giantess of such spectacular scrawniness that she was known in some quarters as Olive Oyle, after Popeye's inamorata. To most of the children though, she was Young Jessica The Witch, and her status as a weaver of spells was confirmed by her manifest power over the remote and aloof Tiger and her skill in conversing with birds. Hardly able to write her name or read Biffo the Bear, she was possessed of a considerable narrative gift, and part of the weird beauty of her stories was that they were always set there, in that very building, and involved characters, or the ancestors of characters, well known to her audience.

She told them how Auld McKinnon on the second storey could never shut his front door because if he did his house would be changed into a jungle and he would be eaten by lions – the same lions that had eaten his wife years and years ago. She told them that she, Jessica, had been personally responsible for the loss of Tam Burke's legs by making a voodoo doll of him and biting its legs off after he had hit her mother with his banjo during a fight in the pub. They knew Mrs McKinnon had died of cancer and Tam Burke had come back from the War without his legs, but they believed her. She told them Tiger could talk even better than Rocky, even better than a human being, but only after midnight when he was alone with her, and then he told her all the secrets he had discovered about everybody during his ghostly slinkings around the building.

She always took their coats and jackets from them and laid them on the bed in the room and at some point in the evening she would steal something from each of their pockets and blame the cat. But when John Findlay lost a shilling, two threepenny bits and a sixpence, and said he didn't believe cats stole money and that he'd tell his mother, she lost her nerve and gave him twelve pennies from Big Jessie's gas money.

She made them do frightening and wonderful things: when they were too politely scared even to look at Joan Reid's withered right arm she induced them all to touch it, and Joan to talk about how it felt to have a useless little stick dangling from her shoulder. Once she persuaded all four boys in the circle – Peter Simpson, Tommy Ruskin, Dom Moore and John Findlay – to loosen their trouser-buttons, but they refused to compare dickie-birds until the girls looked away and even then they grew faint-hearted and spent five minutes fruitlessly daring one another before buttoning up again.

Since none of the boys of her own age would have been seen associating with her, she had few outlets for her ripening sexuality beyond titillating the younger children by sitting with her legs raised and flagrantly parted, or witnessing their excitement when she showed them naked-lady cards from a pack she had found in Fat Alan's drawer, or encouraging them to brush against the soft bulges of her chest through her thin cotton dress.

The evening gatherings remained fairly infrequent occurrences, not only because Jessica had to be in a receptive mood, but because the children, although none was expressly banned from visiting the house on the top landing, were aware of their parents' vague unease about the Brass family, and felt uncomfortable about crossing the threshold. Most nights, Big Jessie was cleaning the billiard hall or enjoying herself at the pub and young Jessica was alone with Tiger and Rocky II.

The cat was intensely interested in the bird, and the bird was no less intensely afraid of the cat. In her eagerness to bring them to a harmonious understanding, Jessica would lift Tiger to the bars of the birdcage and push his nose towards the occupant, whose mad fear contrasted with the cat's air of mild boredom and persuaded her that the problem lay in a simple misapprehension: that Rocky simply saw Tiger as being like other cats – a sworn enemy of his tribe. It was that look of benign uninterest, wholly feigned but never allowed to slip even for a moment, that fooled the girl. Forever caressing and kissing each of her companions separately, she was distressed that Rocky's apparent incivility should hinder the development of a proper loving threesome. She applied herself more vigorously to the task of bringing them together. In the face of Rocky's unwavering refusal to leave his cage if Tiger was in the room, she was forced to take him out and lower him to the floor in her hand. And always it was the same: Tiger would lie relaxed on the linoleum, yawning and looking complaisantly unexcited by the nearness of the trembling and desperately frightened bird: and the bird, the instant Jessica opened her hand, would fly in a blue blurr of terror to the far end of the clothes-pulley, where he would sit cringing until the monster was gone.

Eventually and inevitably, Tiger's patience bore fruit. Jessica, after an hour of assiduous ambassadorship one Friday evening, became irritated with Rocky, and carried him to within an inch of the cat's nose. Unwary in her annoyance with the bird, she was in no position to observe that Tiger was not this time yawning, or blinking, or relaxed, but tensed and even trembling a little. He watched as her fingers began to open, and before the bird was released he thrust out his left paw and sank the claws into the feathers of the right wing. Jessica withdrew her hand and he clamped the bird to the floor.

Rocky's squawks merely strengthened Jessica's annoyance.

'Don't be so stupit, burd,' she said. 'He's no wanting tae hurt you – just say hello and you'll be aw right.'

Tiger cocked his head to one side and looked at the wildly flapping bird with an expression less bored, but hardly more threatening, than before.

'Noo don't hurt him, Tiger, he's getting a bit feart,' Jessica said, and doubt began to creep into her voice.

Tiger, still holding Rocky by the right wing, eased himself closer and held his free paw, claws spread, just above his prisoner's head. He released the wing and as Rocky began to rise he slapped down on the small blue head and fixed it in his claws.

Jessica saw that her plan had miscarried, and tried to part them. Tiger withdrew willingly enough, and the budgie, suddenly freed, rose at a sharp angle, and, with blind violent panic, crashed into the underside of the mantelpiece. He dropped straight down past the grill of the fire and landed on the narrow iron platform at the front of the range. There was a squawking and a singeing of feathers, then he flopped off into the hearth, spun twice around and stopped, dead as a dish-cloth.

Jessica put her head gently on Tiger's back, and together they looked at the body.

'Oh-oh,' she said. 'That's another budgie deid. My mammy'll be really flaming this time.' She looked Tiger in the eye, and when she spoke again the reproach was mild. 'You shouldnae have patted him so hard, you silly bugger – you frightened him to death.'

She leaned over and lifted the tiny singed body from the tiles, wrinkling her nose at the smell. The practicalities of disposing of it quickly cancelled her incipient grief. She thought first of the lavatory, but she had always been afraid to visit in the dark, and the memory of Rocky I's stubbornly buoyant feathers still haunted her. So she turned to Tiger.

'Here,' she said, laying the body in front of him. 'You might as well eat the wee bastit up.'

Tiger was loathe to offend Jessica, but devouring the dead charred thing was the very least of his thoughts. He gave it a disdainful sniff, then stepped carefully over it and went to the door. Jessica, knowing well what his miaow signified, let him out.

She was grateful now for her heaped, furnace-hot fire. She took the long poker and dug out a hollow in the roaring mass of coal, then, approaching as near as she could without scorching her hands, she threw the body in and filled up the hole with fresh fuel. Cunningly she went to the window and opened it about six inches at the top. The story that Big Jessie heard when she arrived home some three hours later was better rehearsed than it needed to be, because she had met The Man With The Painted Heid for the very first time in the pub that night and had kissed him at the pub door and again at the closemouth and was in love and had hardly a thought to spare for lost budgies.

'He'll be a pure gonner, the wee thing,' she said, looking up at the space and at the darkness beyond it. 'The sparrows get them when they fly oot the windae like that. The wee bastits are jealous of the nice colours.'

When Big Jessie brought home Rocky III and a couple of weeks later The Man With The Painted Heid, they said she was looking for a change in her life because Rocky III was white and The Man With The Painted Heid was skinny.

Nobody knew who The Man With The Painted Heid really was, and nobody liked him. He was exotically tall, six-foot-two, and he habitually stood or sat with his back to a wall, not because he was wary of assassins' bullets, like Wild Bill Hickok, but because he wanted no-one to see up close the half-circle of boot-polish he painted on the nape of his neck to simulate hair. He wore grey suits and an expensive grey gabardine cap that he hoped would keep the secret of his spotless ivory crown. With his soft white long-fingered hands and his smooth Americanized accent, he gave off an air of never having worked beyond a few wheelings and dealings on the telephone or at the backs of lorries. Variously they reported him to be English, Italian, American or German, and to clock in at any age between thirty and sixty-five. And he drank brandy, which he called cognac. The fact that he stood in brazen contrast to Fat Alan in almost every department was enough, they said, to turn Big Jessie's head.

She began to appear on the stairs wearing nylons and high-heels and lipstick, and took to drinking gin and tonic instead of stout.

And in truth, she was a woman transformed. His whiteness and his oily voice and his slender soft hands gave him, as far as Big Jessie was concerned, a filmstar otherness; sleeping one night with Gable, the next with Grant, the next with Astaire, she shed half her forty years and neglected young Jessica more shamelessly than ever.

For Jessica, the coming of The Man With The Painted Heid brought to an end a blissful period when her mother loved her and she had a new budgie. The very air in the fourth house, fourth landing turned sour, and both she and Rocky III, in sullen alliance, went to the bad.

From the beginning it had been clear that Rocky III would never be a talker, and that his main accomplishment would be biting. Big Jessie lost a small piece of finger in her first and only attempt to stroke his breast, and young Jessica's lips were hideously and comprehensively bruised before she finally conceded that kissing was not the route to his budgie-heart. The single redeeming feature of his psychotic personality was his scrupulous impartiality: he was a bird who attacked everything. He mangled the bars of his cage, making it impossible to shut him in; he demolished his wooden perch and left his trapeze a twisted heap of wreckage on the floor; he soared to the unassailable safety of the clothes-pulley with clumps of the gasman's hair in his beak; and he saw off the swift and deadly Tiger in no more than three fell swoops. Even in his indolent moments he was actively destructive – from the end of the pulley he could stretch his wonderfully elastic neck and pick the plaster from the wall, and within a week he had created a gaping hole under the ceiling and a festering heap of plaster-powder behind the sink, where Big Jessie never cleaned.

'He'll maybe settle doon,' she said, two weeks into their ordeal. 'Mind you, if he doesnae he'll demolish the whole building, the wee fucker.'

For young Jessica, staring in wonder while Rocky III chewed the wall, the idea was irresistible.

'Ha, ha – imagine that, Mammy, a wee toatie burd pulling doon a great big building. That's a rerr laugh, so it is!'

'Ha, ha,' said Big Jessie.

In any other house Rocky's depredations would have been quickly stopped and the worker of them duly strangled and dumped in the midden, but the Brasses, even the unsavoury male half of the family, had always had a doctrinaire adherence to the view that, as children need play, so animals need exercise; and need had to be satisfied for the wicked as well as for the virtuous. Rocky III might then have found his niche in history as The Bird That Demolished A Building, had it not been for the intervention of The Man With The Painted Heid.

Big Jessie, all awash with sexual discovery, changed utterly, and became plasticine in his clever white hands. With insinuating fingers and a voice whose very softness carried an assumption of command, he subdued her in a manner that would have confounded any of her previous lovers, who had been, to a man, brutal blusterers.

'This will have to stop, right now,' he would say, or 'You'll have to buck up your ideas a bit, baby,' or 'That kid stays up too late – put her to bed.' And although he never raised an assistant hand, the house became as tidy and as quiet as himself.

It was hatred of The Man With The Painted Heid that forced young Jessica to circumvent her fear and continue, with the aid of chocolate, to court the budgie. She suffered in her attempts, for not even chocolate could taint the purity of Rocky III's malevolence; but after a while, bruised and bleeding though she was, she was able to convince herself that the pact was signed, that she and the bird were, if not exactly friends, allies united by their detestation of a common enemy.

The chances of final success for the alliance were slim: The Man With The Painted Heid was not an animal-lover, and a budgie that bit people and destroyed buildings could enter into his scheme of things only as vermin to be exterminated at the earliest opportunity. Both Big Jessie and young Jessica sensed this, and each lived in daily fear of the soft command: that bird will have to go.

Sex was the cause of it, in the end.

After a good Friday night at the pub Big Jessie and The Man With The Painted Heid had made loud love into the small hours. Then, excited by the combination of Saturday-morning sunshine and recollections of the night gone by, they did not dress when they got up. Big Jessie kept on her frilly yellow nightgown, his present to her, and he slipped into his grey flannel dressing-gown. They looked at the unwanted Jessica scooping up her cornflakes, then stared at each other across the table, and he picked up the message from Big Jessie's eyes.

'Is there a matinée at the pictures this morning?' he asked in a casual voice.

'Aye, the Casino,' said Big Jessie, turning her gaze pointedly to Jessica. 'It's they cartoons and that Captain Marvel, isn't it, hen?'

'Aye. It's every Saturday morning,' said Jessica, wondering what their game was.

The Man With The Painted Heid went into the bedroom and came out with money.

'Here,' he said, placing a coin on the table in front of Jessica. 'There's a half-dollar – away and get yourself a box of Maltesers and go and see the pictures.'

Jessica was desperately suspicious, but the prospect of chocolate and of a rare visit to the cinema justified a truce. She took the money and went. When Big Jessie returned from seeing her out of the door, The Man With The Painted Heid was already reclining on the sofa, beckoning. She snuggled up in his lap and kissed him. He still had twenty-two of his own teeth, and his kisses were thrillingly uninhibited. He kissed her neck and bit her ears and cupped her breast in his hand through the gauzy nightgown and she began to wriggle.

They parted for a moment, panting, and she said, 'Let us kiss your heid, go on, I really want to kiss it.'

'Oh no you don't, baby doll, it's too early for that, you've got to work for that.'

'Aw come on, I'm dying to kiss it again. I love your heid, it's that white and shiny.'

She put her hand on the skip of his cap, threatening to pull it off, though they both knew she would never have dared. She kissed his nose, and he relented.

'OK, doll, seeing as you're no everybody.'

He took the cap off and laid it on the sofa beside them and bent his head forwards for her to admire his smooth dome.

'You're the only body in the world gets to see that,' he said, solemnly.

'I want to kiss it.'

'Later, baby.'

'Aw please.'

'No.'

'Aw don't be rotten. I want to kiss it and lick it, every single wee bit of it.'

'Right. You asked for it. Kneel down there.'

She knelt on the floor between his knees and he bowed his head again.

'It's spotless,' she said.

'Now count to three and kiss it. Just the once, for starters.'

She shut her eyes. 'One . . . two . . .'

She opened her eyes when he screamed, and fell backwards when he sprang, still screaming, to his feet with Rocky III clinging to his head. The talons were anchored firmly in the scalp and the beak that twisted metal and sliced through wood and made rubble of walls was hammering with ferocious abandon on his naked white pate.

Jessie lay back helpless, watching him as he leapt about the room. He finally managed to catch the bird a blow with one of his flailing arms, and it fluttered up to the pulley. Its white breast-feathers were spotted with blood.

In his agony and grief, The Man With The Painted Heid let fall his mask of otherness, and lost his style completely. What issued from his lips was no longer American or English or Italian or German but pure Govan.

'Oh Jesus Christ, my heid, my heid, I'm bleeding to death, so I am. That fucking burd, I'll kill it, I'll guzzle the bastit!'

Seeing Rocky out of reach, he turned to Big Jessie. 'Whit you daeing lying there like a deid coo? Away'n get us disinfectant afore my heid festers.'

'What kind of disinfectant? I've no got nothing like that.'

'Well fucking get some – it'll fester.'

She stood up, a little shocked at his language, but hard pushed not to laugh. 'Margot Connolly'll have some. She's got things like that.'

'Oh God, hurry up, I'll get bloody lockjaw,' he said, taking off his dressing-gown and passing it to her.

She did not hurry. She was thinking, as she shuffled along the landing in her battered slippers: young Jessica had always insisted that dogs and cats and birds were better than men, and she was beginning to understand what she meant. By the time she shuffled back with a half-full bottle of Pine, having lingered awhile at Margot's door to tell her the story of the morning's events, he had washed his head under the tap and was inspecting the damage in the mirror. He was still in a state of some shock, but had recovered his accent and with it a little of his authority.

'Look at that.' He turned from the mirror and stooped to give her a view. 'Look what that damned bird's done to my head.'

The desecration of the pristine dome was, she had to admit, a sorry sight. It looked, that dome, as if it had done service as a battlefield in some murderous War of the Ants. Rocky's clawmarks formed two distinct rosettes, and above them, towards the back of the skull, was an area of welt that ran through the spectrum from bright scarlet to deep purple.

'If that festers I could die,' he moaned, and Big Jessie thought again what a snivelling wretched thing a man could be.

'Here, I'll dab it with this,' she said.

He sat down and she sponged the Pine on to his wounds and he squealed with the fresh agony of it.

'There – you'll probably live, and your wee heid'll soon be as lovely as ever it was.'

The hint of irony in her voice was new, and he looked up at her from under his bushy eyebrows. As if sensing that his look, normally sufficient in itself to establish dominance, was lacking in potency, he stood up and garnered all his reserves of male power in order to issue the proclamation:

'That Bird Will Have To Die.'

The cinema belched the children out at half-past eleven and young Jessica came home hot with excitement and sticky with chocolate and already terrified that she might not be allowed to go next week: Billy Batson was hanging upside down in a metal-lined room, unable to shout shazaam because his mouth was gagged, and the villain Sylvana had unscrewed a valve to release fifty thousand gallons of water. The water had reached Billy Batson's nose. She burst into the house, ready to tell Big Jessie the story, but was immediately hit by the frost.

'What's the matter, Mammy?' She glanced up at the pulley, then across at the cage, and seeing them both empty she cried out, 'Where's wee Rocky? What've yous done tae him?'

Big Jessie looked at The Man With The Painted Heid, now restored to his customary grey suavity, and said nothing. He too was silent, and Jessica clenched her fists and pressed them against her cheeks.

'Where is he?' she shouted.

'He's in his cage, hen, go and see.'

She went to the cage, and looked in, and gasped.

Rocky III was lying on the floor, on his back, with his feet in the air. His wings were trussed to his sides by several strands of parcel twine.

'What's the matter, Mammy, is he hurted?'

'He dies at noon,' said The Man With The Painted Heid.

Jessica roared, and Big Jessie hugged her.

'Don't greet, hen,' she said. 'Yon was a rotten burd – I'll get you a new one.'

'I don't want a new one, I want Rocky.'

'We'll call the new one Rocky. This is a rotten one – you should see what he's went and done.' She turned to The Man With The Painted Heid. 'Show her what the wee bastit done to your heid,' she said.

His hand twitched upwards to his cap, but he shook his head.

'He's made a right mess of your uncle's heid – you want to see it, it's really scandalous, so it is.' She saw hope in diverting attention from the bound bird to the wounded man.

'He's no my uncle,' Jessica protested.

'He is – he's your new uncle.'

'Uncle my arse – he's just a silly old cunt wi a painted heid!'

'Jessica!' Big Jessie was shocked. Until now Jessica, despite years of exposure to Fat Alan's coarseness, had remained one of the most temperate-tongued of the tenement children. 'You've no to talk aboot him like that, that burd nearly kilt him!'

'Good. I weesht it had. I weesht it would shout shazaam and fly oot of that cage and kill the big bastit really.'

'Shut up now, Jessica, that's terrible.'

'Yes, young woman, I think we've heard enough from you.' Sensing the first serious crisis in his reign in the fourth house, fourth landing, The Man With The Painted Heid rose to his full six-foot-two and spoke from deep in his chest. He succeeded, to his relief, in making a silence, and filled it with a final magisterial pronouncement.

'At five to twelve that oven goes on, and at twelve o'clock precisely that bird goes in.' He stressed the last deadly preposition by stamping his foot and creating another tense silence. It was quarter to twelve. Jessica fell against her mother's breast and sobbed; Rocky III chirped feebly at the ceiling. The Man With The Painted Heid was pleased with himself.

For five minutes the only sounds were the muffled sobs of young Jessica and an occasional weak chirp from the condemned cell. Then, at ten to twelve, there was a kick at the door.

'That'll be our Maureen,' said Big Jessie, freeing herself from Jessica's tight embrace. 'She said she'd bring us some meat this weekend.'

She opened the door and Maureen, her sister from Springburn, poured in, covered in half-plucked chickens. Maureen was hardly five-foot tall, and her permanent stoop made her look even shorter. Every Saturday she made the round of her friends and relations distributing largesse in the form of meat that she picked up from the market where her man, Gerry, loaded and unloaded refrigerated lorries.

'Hello everybody – it's only daft Maureen, don't put your best suits on,' she said. 'I thought yous might fancy another bit of chicken for your Sunday dinner.' She extracted two birds from her bundle and dropped them on the table. Then she noticed the atmosphere. 'What's the matter wi yous then? It's like a bloody funeral in here.'

Young Jessica howled and ran to her favourite aunt for comfort. Big Jessie explained, and Maureen laughed.

'Silly buggers, yous cannae gas a wee burd just for biting heids. Christ, we're black and blue wi oor birds – and wir dugs as well, they bite the legs aff you every time you go in the hoose.'

Young Jessica, who had always liked her Auntie Maureen, adored her now. The Man With The Painted Heid shuffled his feet and felt the embarrassment of the mean-spirited come face to face with the utterly-giving.

'Well Maureen,' he said, nodding towards the cage, 'if you want to take that bird off our hands, you're welcome. But I warn you, he's a vicious wee bugger – look what he's done to the wall.'

It was not easy for her to incline her head at the angle required for a full inspection of the damage. She gave a hurried dismissive glance and made a farting noise with her lips before she spoke:

'My wee Joey could beat that any day, and he's got a broken tail. And wee Billy's ten times worser nor him. And the dugs chewed the legs right aff my new coffee table.' She went across to Rocky's cage. 'Gie's him,' she said, reaching in and plucking him out with the easy confidence of the uncompromising animal-lover. 'He'll be a wee pal for Joey and Billy.' She dropped the trussed and unprotesting Rocky III into her coat pocket and patted him gently through the cloth. 'There, there, son,' she said, 'you come hame wi your daft Auntie Maureen.' Then she turned to young Jessica. 'You can come and visit him at your auntie's any time you like, hen, OK?'

'Ta you're a real pal, Auntie Maureen.'

'Right well, I'll love yous and leave yous, there's still aboot eight burds to deliver, and I've a bit of ham here for Old Sloag.'

The Man With The Painted Heid packed his case two weeks later and went to live with his aged mother in Govan. Big Jessie and young Jessica went to Taylor's pet shop together and bought a hen bird and called it Teenie. Rocky III lived for ten more happy years, happily biting moving and unmoving things in Maureen's Springburn house, and young Jessica, for a joke, took to calling her mother's sister Auntie Shazaam.

Tiger

Haecceity doesn't trouble me a lot among the chimney-pots. At other times, in other places, yes, I'm as thirled to the Thisness and Nowness of things as the next cat, and it's for that reason that I would argue that the profligate Realism of my flights on the slates can hardly be said to compromise my Scotist credentials. Up there, let me confess it at once, all slates are slate-essence and there are no chimneys, just Chimney, and I lose myself in nine-lived flight, in pure poise, in glorious Gleichgewicht.

I do worry about these things, even here, where mice are as plentiful as November raindrops. Worry, irrational though it is, I regard as a legitimate and fruitful element in my commerce with things visible and invisible: fatness is fine, but there are dangers. Sparky might be said to exemplify some of them: the easy lure of the dustbin has, in his case, corrupted a mind that belongs, potentially, to the highest order. Set his rather brutish rummagings against my elegant meanderings through the full rich meadow of the -isms and you might be forgiven for assigning us to different spheres, to separate monads so determinedly windowless that intercourse of any but the grossest kind would be out of the question. That, however, would be a sad misrepresentation of our relationship. We talk. We exchange. We are by no means the polar opposites that our favoured habitats might suggest: I am a being of the upper regions, who intimately lives with clouds; he dwells in dustbins.

I say we talk, but it should not be assumed from this

that we spend any time together. Quite the reverse: his dusty step, trodden upon two thousand times daily by the Sweaty Ones, and his hot maggoty dustbin, are as distasteful to me as my rainwashed airy slates are inaccessible to him. Our paths cross seldomer now than in the past, when he was more mobile, and when they do, alas, we bristle – an atavistic reaction all the more distressing because we each recognize that our position here among the teeming masses of rats and mice and Sweaty Ones imposes responsibilities, among which the maintenance of a dignified demeanour at all times and in the face of all provocation is not the least important. The rats, though numerous, present no great problem. With Sparky they have no contact beyond a timorous squeak or two and a prudent retreat – testimony to past rather than present exploits, since his state of well-fed indolence and near toothlessness obviates almost all threat to their bodily welfare. The generation that knew him as Neckbreaker has long since passed on, but reputations die hard. From me they keep a distance born of dislike, distaste and distrust: sentiments which I, of course, unstintingly reciprocate. The mice, being beneath the notice of either Sparky or the rats, are unnegotiably all mine.

All mine: mice, slates, chimney-pots, sunshine – I think I can be forgiven my occasional lapses into solipsism.

It is, inevitably, in our approach to the Sweaty Ones that Sparky and I find ourselves most implacably at odds. It is not that his contempt for them is less intense than mine – God forbid that I should reproach him with softness – only that he is distressingly prone to let it sink into mere anger. He snarls at them, barks at them, on occasion bites them. I think he has problems with his digestion. I have tried to explain to him that his other approach – his affectation of cringing obeisance in order to beg scraps from them – is a more permissible and infinitely more powerful means of asserting his superiority, but he remains stupidly and stubbornly deaf to my advice. What upsets me most is his perverse insistence on attacking the very ones who might be deemed worthy of some interest, perhaps even some respect. Jessica, for example. I warm myself at their embers, take titbits from their tables, allow myself in my more indulgent moments to be stroked – but only in the case of Jessica is the purity of my loathing for them a little moderated. And it is a mark of Sparky's intellectual coarseness that he should have selected this sweetest and warmest of them as his special target, and that he should refuse to respond to my queries on the matter, other than to bristle and to change the subject. I have once or twice been forced to the conclusion that Sparky, having reluctantly accepted that I occupy, in existential terms, a higher niche, and having rightly divined some affinity between me and her alone among the Sweaty Ones, has unconsciously chosen her as the focus for his rankling sense of grievance. There was a time, perhaps, in his sprightlier middle-age, when he might have been amenable to reason in an affair such as this, but as is often the case with his kind, age has brought not wisdom, but crustiness. As it is, I try to recompense Jessica by paying her rather more small attentions than she might, in normal circumstances, be thought to deserve. These amount in winter to almost nightly intercourse, and it would be a failure in candour for me to suggest other than that the pleasure gained is entirely mutual.

Jessica, left alone in the house while her elders carouse downstairs, heaps coal on the fire and sits with her back against the sofa and her legs raised and parted. She beckons with her hands and I approach. She strokes me gently, lingeringly, and I close my eyes and enjoy the rival attractions of hearth and fire-warmed muscular thighs.

She draws me slowly in still stroking my back tenderly, to where she smells all smotheringly sweet, and for the moment she, poor child, forgets her fears, and I forget Slate.

The Stinky Ocean

The railway was a neat black scar through the heart of the Cuddies Park. On one side passengers had a view of the camouflaged facade of the Chemical Works, on the other, a glimpse and a whiff of the Stinky Ocean. Forty yards diametrically opposite the place where the Ocean lapped the railway embankment the slope of Jack's Mountain began and rose to a summit of a hundred feet, the highest point in the Cuddies Park, before dropping somewhat more precipitantly to the grey chalky desert known as the Salt Waste, which extended to the canal bank.

The whole area was badlands: children drowned in the canal, broke their necks on the Mountain, swallowed disease in the Waste and in the sooty clotted grass of the Park.

One drowned in the Ocean itself, and his ghost haunted the last two years of Sniffer O'Hara's life.

It was not his sapsy voice or his never-quite-focused eyes or his relentless green-running nose, but a something that was more than the mere combination of these things, that established Sniffer in the eyes of the tenement – though he was manifestly not half as deranged as a dozen or more other inhabitants – as the king of the dafties. His nine-year-old playmates esteemed his strength and his generosity as the drunken hangers-on in the meadhalls had esteemed their ring-giving warrior-kings, and they envied his limitless talent for attracting disaster. He transformed the dullest of excursions into a safari, and told stories they could laugh with, and laugh at, in a delightful mixture of contempt and admiration. Behind his daft eyes, he seemed somehow miraculously in touch with, yet detached from, his own daftness – able to mock it and tell stories against it, stories that always ended, after labyrinthine twistings and turnings, in the same way: 'See me, see daft – I'm a daft bastit, so I am.'

Some of his accidents had become lore, and he basked royally in their fame, recounting them with disarming insight into his own and the world's folly to squatting groups of children under the gasmantle on the second landing on winter evenings when the wind howled up the stairwell.

'Tell us the one aboot . . . tell us the one aboot . . .' And he would weigh up their competing demands and wait for silence before beginning.

He led Wee Pete Simpson and Andrew Doherty to the Cuddies Park on a damp morning in the summer holidays. They found sticks and some string and roped themselves together – Sniffer in front – to climb the south face of Jack's Mountain. They rested at the top, looking out across the Ocean, then southwards over the land, seeing the stylized daubs on the Chemical Works as what they were supposed to have been in the eyes of Nazi pilots – hills and valleys and woods. There was a perpetual clutter of junk in and around the Ocean, and when they turned northwards again Sniffer's trained eye was able to pick out from among the boxes and prams and bicycle frames the thing that most met their needs – a battered wardrobe.

'Come on, gang, we'll be the Crimson Pirate!' he said, leading the other two in a charge down the north slope to the edge of the Ocean. 'This can be wir pirate ship.' He kicked the side of the wardrobe, testing its strength and found it adequate for a voyage to the Spanish Main. They hauled it to the water. It had no doors and its front was badly rotted, but beyond that it seemed tight enough, and the slow oozings of stinking slimy water that came through when they launched it did not impress them as dangerous.

Sniffer lifted the two smaller boys in and gave a final push which took him knee-deep into the sludge before he boarded his vessel. They punted themselves using their mountaineering sticks, then adjusted their weights until the ship felt stable, and allowed themselves to drift into the middle of the Ocean.

'I'm the Crimson Pirate,' Sniffer said. 'And Pete, you're Deadeye Dick, and Andy, you're just the trusty cabin-boy because you're only quite wee. Ahoy, ye varlets!'

He made sea-music, wide-blue-sky-music punctuated by the heaving rhythm of the anchor and chain and the full-sailed straining of ropes and timbers. 'Da-da- darrum! Da-da-darrum! Darrum darrum darrummmmm!'

They played pirates with controlled violence, mindful of the unseaworthiness of their craft. Deadeye Dick murmured of mutiny and was given twenty lashes and threatened with the plank. The trusty cabin-boy saved the captain's life and was rewarded with a doubloon and promoted to second mate. Then, oppressed a little by the heaviness of the damp misty summer morning and the sickly fumes of the Ocean, they settled back against the gunwhales and relaxed, while Sniffer hummed out the last triumphant chords. They were quiet for a while, letting the wardrobe spin slowly in the mysterious Ocean currents. It was a bleak, birdless world, their Spanish Main. Sounds were muffled, reduced to the distant hum of traffic and to Sniffer's snorts as he drew his sleeve across his nose.

'Tell us a story, Michael,' said Wee Pete, using his leader's Sunday name as he knew he must. 'Tell's the one aboot the matches, be a pal!'

'Aye, be a pal, Michael,' Andrew chimed in, 'the one aboot the matches.'

'Right well, but yous have to be dead dead dead dead dead quiet.'

They were quiet, and he began.

'Right well. You know how I smoke quite a lot, don't I? Well no as much as I used to, but quite a lot still. Well my mammy doesnae know I smoke and she'd pure murder me if she found oot, so I keep my matches loose in my back pocket, so's she willnae hear them rattling aboot, right? So one day we're up at the Garngad swings, a whole load of us – who was aw there?'

'I was there Michael, smart as a brush,' said Wee Pete.

'I wasnae,' said Andrew, sadly.

'That's right, Petey boy, you was there, dead right you was, you seen the lot, so you did. Anyways, we were playing on that joywheel thing – no the one wi the flerr on it, the other one.'

'Wi the bars.'

'Aye, the bars you hing fae. Goes roon like lightning, so it does. Anyways, we're playing on this joywheel . . .'

'Who?' asked Andy. 'Who aw was there?'

'Me and my pals, you daft cunt – noo shut up and listen, will you? Anyways, Big Davy, he runs like the wind, yous know him, don't yous? He starts shoving the wheel, and we're aw hingin' on the bars and it gets faster and faster and faster and you couldnae see fuck all, it was aw just a blur so it was, and we was aw shouting and Big Davy shoved harder and harder. Christ, it was that fast you thought help we're gonnae fly aff this thing. Then Big Davy hung on as well and the thing was that fast it took hours and hours to slow doon and when it was nearly stopped I wanted to get aff, so I just let my arse drap doon a wee bit, just a wee toatie bit, but Christ, it touched the grun and the next thing BANG, there's a fucking great puff of smoke and my fucking bum's roasting and I jumps up that fast my heid hits the bar and I split it open but

I never even noticed it, my bum was that sore. Christ, there's aboot thirty matches there aw blazing up at the same time. I was running roon the swings shouting my heid aff: "Mammy Daddy, Mammy Daddy, my bum's aw burnt, my bum's aw burnt!" Then I ran aw the way doon Tower Street screaming blue murder . . .'

At this point the others, in a well-practised routine, joined with him in his chant:

'Mammy Daddy Mammy Daddy my bum's burnt aff my bum's burnt aff!'

And they rocked the wardrobe with their laughing, and when they were quiet again, clutching their sides, Sniffer reminded them, as he always did, that he had needed five stitches in his head as well as ointment on his bum, though his mother thought ointment was bad for burns. Then he finished: 'See me, see daft – I'm a daft bastit, so I am.'

They sat silently reliving the story in their heads for a while, a serene four minutes before the disaster struck that would be re-enacted nightly behind Sniffer's wide silly eyes – though the telling of it under the gaslight would be for Peter Simpson, the smug innocent party, to enjoy.

It was Wee Pete who began it, in truth. He leaned his back on the side of the wardrobe and, staring up at the dark brooding mass of Jack's Mountain, said aloud to himself: '"The Black Hills of Dakota".'

The others, understanding, tuned in.

'That was a stoating picture that,' said Andrew Doherty.

'Great,' Sniffer agreed. 'I seen it three times – once on Monday, once on Tuesday and once on Wednesday. That Doris Day's great, so she is.'

'I like Gabby Hayes,' said Pete.

'He wasnae in it you daft bastit,' said Sniffer.

'Don't care. He's my favourite. And I like the songs.'

'What song did you like the best, Peter?' Andrew Doherty knew the answer well enough – they had had the same discussion a dozen times.

'Huh.' Peter snorted prophylactically, dismissing any possible alternatives before he made his pronouncement. '"The Deadwood Stage" – nae bother.'

Sniffer's knuckles, lying atop the gunwhales, whitened, but he said nothing, allowing Pete and Andrew to wallow awhile in concord.

'Christ aye – that bit aboot the fancy cargo and that whipcrackaway and that – smashing.'

'"The Black Hills of Dakota" is smashing tae, but "The Deadwood Stage" is the best a mile.'

And while the crew tossed out favourite episodes and sang snatches of favourite songs, the captain simmered and sniffed and gripped the sides of the ship until finally he could bear it no longer. He spoke quietly, tentatively, as if trying to withdraw his remark even as he made it, and before he finished it he was already clenching his fists for the defence of his freedom of opinion:

'Well I liked "Secret Love".'

The shock was even more profound than he had expected: it seemed the distant traffic stopped to register its amazement; the Chemical Works chimney and the lowering mass of Jack's Mountain itself seemed to lean forward, menacing in their incredulity. He felt his skin prickle with shame, and clenched his fists tighter and wished the Ocean would swallow him up.

'What?'

And though he had been rehearsing this very moment in his head, Sniffer could not take up the challenge directly, could not repeat his shocking utterance. Instead, he leaned forward, and shook his fist at the younger boys.

'What do yous know aboot it anyway? I've seen the picture three times, you daft bastits.'

But they had the advantage, and were not to be shaken by his fourteen-year-old bluster.

'Deh – deh – darreh – deh. He likes "Secret Love".'

They clung together uninhibited in their mockery, and sang his cissiness to the leaden sky:

O – o – o – once – I had a secret love
That lived within the heart of me – ee – ee . . .

'Shut up yous! Fucking shut up or I'll lamp yous, so I will.'

But they were borne on a pitiless tide of scorn, and his threats meant nothing:

All too soon my se – e – e – cret love
Became impatient to be free – ee – ee.

'Shut up or else.' Sniffer half rose from his perch on the side of the wardrobe, tearful in his rage, but reluctant, as he always was, to strike one of the smaller boys. He tried to distract them by switching back to the Crimson Pirate:

'Da-da-darrum, da-da-darrum! Ahoy, yous varlets, haul the mainsails, weigh the anchor, we're bound for the Spanish Main!'

He was partially successful: the others became pirates again – but mocking, half-mutinous pirates. Andrew Doherty, who secretly knew all the words, wove "Secret Love" into his pirate rhythm, singing as he punted the wardrobe further across the Ocean:

N – ow – ow I shouted from the highest hill,
Even told the golden da – ff – o – dil,
At last my heart's an open door . . .

'Shut up you! Shut up ya lubber!' Unable to hit the

smaller boy in the serious quarrel, Sniffer could now incorporate the blow into their game. He slapped Andrew Doherty on the shoulder. More push than blow, and by no means viciously delivered, it was nevertheless enough. The smaller boy stumbled forwards under the shock of it, caught his shins on the side of the wardrobe, and plunged head first into the Stinky Ocean.

He did not, by some perverse providence, break his skull or gouge out his eyes on any of the metal wreckage with which the pond was strewn, but splashed cleanly into three feet of water and bobbed up again, panicking as his feet refused to find a solid bottom. The others smelled death and panicked in unison, pushing the wardrobe away from his groping hands lest he should drag them down with him. They reached indecisively towards him, then drew back as they felt the wardrobe tilt. Wee Pete pushed frantically on his stick, aiming for the nearest bank. They snagged on an upturned pram and Andrew Doherty, falling towards them and keeping afloat with a desperate dog-paddle, caught the side of the wardrobe.

'Christ, he'll sink us – get him aff!' Peter Simpson shouted.

In his panic Sniffer was frozen, unable to move his weight across to the place where Andrew was clinging. He lay back, keeping his head and shoulders pressed against the floor, then stretched his long legs towards the clutching fingers. He thumped his heels up and down on the edge, trying to dislodge the fingers. Then he found the range and struck once, twice, three times. Andrew Doherty screamed, opened his hands, and went under.

Suddenly released, the wardrobe was propelled towards the bank, and Peter was able to ground it with a last push on his stick. They scrambled ashore and staggered up the side of Jack's Mountain and without looking back passed over the summit and down towards the road.

Andrew Doherty, submerging for the third time, ran out of luck: his eyes caught the fork of a bicycle frame and his mouth opened to let in the Stinky Ocean.

Peter was framing his story as they ran for the street.

'You murdered him, so you did,' he said to Sniffer.

'Fucking shut up, I did not.'

'You did sot, I seen you. But I won't tell.'

'Fucking shut up – we've got to get help.'

They crossed the wooden canal bridge and came to the open door of the blacksmith's forge, where they had often, in happier times, lounged around to watch the horses being shod or the great iron shoes being hammered into shape. Tam Walters, the smith, was pumping up his furnace.

Sniffer found his voice first: 'Mister, mister, there's a boy fell in the Stinky Ocean, hurry up!'

'What?'

'It's wir pal – he's drooning.'

Their sincerity was not to be doubted. Tam Walters dropped his bellows.

'You show me where,' he said to Sniffer. 'And you,' turning to Pete, 'run to the police office and tell them.' Sniffer blanched at the thought of what Pete might say.

'He fell in, he just fell,' he shouted at the world, as he led the blacksmith back across Jack's Mountain.

From the top they could see only the flat lifeless water of the Ocean. Their ripples, and those of the dying boy, had spent themselves on the shore. They went down to the wardrobe.

'Right,' the blacksmith said. 'I'll lie across this and you shove me oot fae the bank.'

'Aboot there,' Sniffer shouted when the wardrobe reached the place where they had abandoned their friend to the Ocean. 'That's where he fell in.'

'Cannae see a bloody thing,' said Tam Walters. He

eased himself into the water, exploring its muddy bottom with his feet and legs.

The police, PC McGlaughlin and young Blake, brought ropes and hooks, and were climbing into their thigh-boots when Tam Walters found the soft yielding bulk of Andrew Doherty. He did not need the tackle, but raised the body by working his right foot under it, easing it across his shin, then catching hold of it in his big powerful hands.

PC McGlaughlin, seeing the gaping socket of Andrew Doherty's right eye, did not even go through the motions of resuscitation. Between them he and Tam carried the dripping thing across Jack's Mountain and down to the ambulance.

Sniffer and Wee Pete were taken to the police station in the squad car. Sniffer was blubbering his guilt and sorrow into a handkerchief supplied by young Blake. Peter, fevered by the morning's events and by the hold he now had over Sniffer, was singing in a smug undertone, directing his voice across the heaving left shoulder of his friend, but making sure it did not carry as far as young Blake:

When we get ho – o – me we're fixing to stay,
So – whipcrackaway, whipcrackaway, whipcrack-away . . .

Baroque

Four of nature's stone tits are visible – the others are obscured by Thalia's tight blonde coiffure. All the women are, of course, naked. The three unlovely specimens in the foreground, two of whom are adorning the plinth with gourds while the third hanky-pankies with a satyr, force the eye upwards to the Graces themselves, who bedeck the statue with cloth and beads. Altogether sweeter these three, though none in her own right entirely satisfies: take the soft smiling profile of Euphrosine, the neat rosy buttocks of Thalia, and the slim arching torso of Aglia (who is, alas, distressingly short in the legs), and you might claim an acceptable composite loveliness. Industry is everywhere more apparent than genius: the panel emanated from the Antwerp studio during its most fruitful period, when the friendship between Peter Paul and Velvet Breughel (son of the great Pieter) was at its height, but the attribution to the two masters is wishful. Notwithstanding some thick fruity moments, it is for the most part a dully symmetrical production, whose dull stone heart is enlivened beyond deserving by Thalia's off-centre and unarguably beautiful arse.

'I could staun here for ever,' Wee Pete Simpson said.

He was a wicked liar, but he meant it when he said that. He worshipped Peter Paul Rubens, and adored Thalia's arse.

He was barred from nearly everywhere: barred from the Carlton for sneaking in without paying; barred from the

Casino for firing an arrow at Randolph Scott, even though it missed; barred from the swimming-pool for having shit-streaked legs; barred from Mr Buchan's sweetshop for stealing penny dainties to give to the younger kids; barred from the No. 8 tram for dropping frogs on the driver's head.

He could stand all these, but he cried bitter hot tears that Sunday when they barred him from the Art Gallery.

The Gallery was a two-and-half-mile trek straight through the city. He went every Sunday, sometimes alone but usually leading a small pack. It was an exciting trek, in three distinct stages: the familiar stretch as far as the bus station, where rival gang members might stone them or window-hanging women throw down oranges or bits of Saturday's leftover spam; the long long splendour of Sauchiehall Street, swept clean, and quiet for the sabbath, where they had competitions to find the most costly ring in the jewellers' windows or the most death-filled picture on the publicity-boards outside the cinemas; the alien elegance of the West End, where thin women rapped on window-panes to drive them off the grass.

The others went for the model ships and the suits of armour and the skinny dirty girls in tight skirts and stiff lacquered curls who hung around the display cases giggling at their own reflections. He went for Rubens. Only the boldest of them ever dared to nudge a girl or even toss a lewd remark at a group of girls. And only Pete, on the rare occasions when he condescended to stay downstairs, was bold enough to break the circle of their girlishness and rakishly announce himself:

'Hi dolls. I'm Pete. Your lucky day.'

Nor was he at a loss when, as sometimes happened, the girls took the initiative.

'Hey you boys, fancy some split tomatoes?'

'Sure doll. Dae yous fancy some sausages?'

Miss Brander said he was a stupid stupid boy and would end up in Barlinnie and it was lucky for him she was there to thrash him three or four times a day; but Wee Pete had class.

The pack was generally nervous about going upstairs to the paintings because there were rarely any girls there and the attendants were stricter and might follow them about to make sure they touched nothing. And anyway, apart from the prancing horses and the naked women, the pictures were less exciting than the ships and guns and stuffed animals. But sometimes if girls were scarce they would follow Pete up the wide stone staircase and he would take them on a conducted tour and tell them which pictures they should like.

He was content, apart from his idiosyncratic devotion to the Graces, to pass on as great those pictures which the Gallery had already distinguished by fencing off: big ones, for the most part.

He lingered over Dali.

'See that? That is the dearest photie in the world.'

'Is not.'

'Is fucking sot. That photie costed hunners and hunners.'

'Well I wouldnae gie them fourpence for it. It's stupit-looking.'

'What dae you mean, stupit-looking? The Pope says it's a sin, that photie. He says they've got tae burn it.'

'Dead right. Look at it. How come he's floating in the air like that? Jesus didnae float aboot in the sky like that.'

'How the fuck dae you know?'

'We got it in school. He never done that.'

'School, Christ. That's Salvador *Dali*, for Christ's sake. That is the dearest photie in the world. You couldnae buy that photie if you saved up for a million years.'

'You're no supposed tae see Jesus's face in pictures. It's

a sin if you see his face, my da told me.'

'I know. They used tae show you his face in the olden days, but. It was aw right then. Salvador Dali's the first man tae make him floating; and curly-haired. That's how it's the dearest photie in the world.'

He showed them the *Man in Armour*.

'Look at that. Stoating, eh?'

'No bad.'

'That's Rembrandt, sonny boy, that's the greatest picture in the world.'

'Thought that Salvador Dali one was the greatest, yey-yey.'

'Naw, stupit-appearance. He's the dearest, but Rembrandt's the greatest.'

'It's helluva dark.'

'That's whit's good aboot it! That's how he's the greatest. In them olden days everybody just done light photies then he done them dark and they aw said, Christ, that's magic, that. He's the greatest that's ever been, nae bother.'

Before the Graces he permitted no argument. When Dom Moore said it was more like Arses than Graces he dug him hard in the ribs with his elbow and threatened to kick him back downstairs.

'I could staun here for ever,' he said.

'Whit one dae you fancy, then?'

'Her in the middle. I just staun here and look at her and look and look and look.'

'Dae you get a big stauner?'

'Smart as a brush. I feel it through my pocket. Look.'

His trouser pockets had lost their lining and he wore no underpants.

'Dirty bastit.'

'I am not. Bare naked's no dirty when it's a real photie in an art gallery. I love that one stretching up as well, her stauning on the guy's back and that, her big long arms and her wee tits. And that guy wi the hoofs, and aw they apples and oranges and that. Wish I could jump right intae it.'

That Sunday he had gone to the Gallery with Dom Moore and John Findlay, and had left them downstairs with the ships while he made straight for the Graces. The room was empty apart from a vulturish attendant who stood poised for pouncing at the first hint of mischief.

He stood with his hands in his pockets, staring, weaving himself into the fantastic fabric of the picture.

His baroque meander took an unvarying route now: from the group perched dangerously on the left-hand tree-trunk, along the shimmering length of the scarlet cloth that was about to drape Nature's head, to the floating cherubs crowning her with a wreath; from them to the muscle-bound satyrs on the right-hand trunk, then down its fruit-laden length to the lecherous pair in the right foreground, and across to the plump nymphs on the left; upward to the fat old satyr and his assistant, and from the top of the ugly old head to the plinth, the statue, the gracious threesome. And as he wandered he slowly lost his attachment to the floorboards, to his own brown and evil-smelling legs, to his hard-pressed mother and his foul-mouthed father and his raucous brothers and sisters; to his very name. The Graces adorned, and he adored, mumbling, and fingering forth through his unlined pockets his love of fat and fruit.

The attendant decided he was harmless, and moved out into the corridor.

He was alone now with Thalia's arse, concentrating his entire being on that and on his swollen dickiebird, which he had unwittingly pulled into his right pocket space, and was absently kneading in the fingers of his right hand.

He could, as he had often said, have stood there for ever, but after five minutes he realized he was not alone any more – was being watched. It was not this in itself that disturbed, but the fact that the watchers were three girls, and they had begun to giggle. They were older than himself – at least thirteen – and dressed in adult fashion, with tight skirts and nylons and high-heeled shoes. Two blondes and one brunette. In his entrancement he did not at once register their corporality, but absorbed them into his vision. Three Graces. Then his eyes focused, and his fingers stopped, and he addressed them.

'Hi dolls. I'm Pete. Your lucky day.'

They giggled.

'How's it gaun then? Whit's your names?'

'Joan and Jacqueline and Dorothy.'

He pointed at the picture.

'Fancy that one there? Fancy that Rubens guy? I think he's rerr. Three wives that guy, nae kidding, three of them.'

'Honest tae God?' Jacqueline was bolder than the others.

'Yup. And that's his three sisters, them three at the bottom. Crossmyheartandhopetodie. Three wives, smart as a brush. That's the three of them in that photie, up there on that statue.'

'Is it really, but?'

'Yup. And they aw took their claes aff and he painted them. Come and see.'

He took his hand from his pocket and reached towards her with a chivalrous turn of his head. Approaching, she noticed first his smell, then in his disarranged trouser pocket, his excitement.

'My God.' She turned to the others. 'Joan, Dorothy, you should see this wee boy!'

They moved in on him, giggling, climbing towards hysteria. He restored himself to comparative decency and fended them off.

'Way yous go, daft bitches.'

'Ugh, he smells aw keichy.'

'Get lost, fucking hoors.'

The attendant, suspicious again, had come back into the room, and Joan ran to him.

'Hey mister, that wee boy swore at us.'

The others joined her.

'He called us effing hoors.'

'And he was playing with hissel, in front of that nudie picture.'

'What?'

'He made Jacqueline look at his thing, so he did.'

'What? Come here, you.'

'I never done nothing, mister, I was just looking at the pictures.'

'Shut up you. I've had my eye on you for a while – you're aye coming in here, looking at they pictures. Well that's your last, you dirty wee swine. You're barred. I should get the polis tae you, frightening these lassies!'

'I never frightened naebody, I was just looking at the photies, honest tae God.'

'Shut up. Come on – oot.'

He pushed Wee Pete out into the corridor, keeping his distance when he too became aware of the smell. At the revolving door he repeated the sentence.

'Right. You're barred for good. Away hame and don't come near here again, and think yoursel bloody lucky I'm no reporting you to the Corporation.'

Dom Moore and John came out and found him tear-stained and abject on the steps.

'Whit's the matter, Petey boy? We were looking everywhere for you – did somebody hit you?'

'I'm barred for ever. The bastit said I swore at these lassies and I didnae. I was just looking at the fucking photies. Fucking Rubens.'

'Was it the Three Graces?'

'Aye.'

'Dirty bastit. You should tell your da – they're no allowed tae bar you fae the Art Gallery, it doesnae belang tae them, they only work there.'

'I know. I'll tell my Maw. I'll tell my big brother, and I'll get the polis tae them, so I will.'

They started the long haul home, and it seemed shorter than usual because they had a theme and an enemy.

'That guy's a real bastit, Pete, and I bet you he knows fuck all aboot photies.'

'I know.' Wee Pete was sniffling.

'You know tons merr nor him about it.'

'Dead fucking right.'

'You know everything aboot they painter guys. Bet he doesnae know fuck all aboot that Salvador Dali. And he works in the place.'

The Job's comfort took effect, and Peter sobbed again.

'Know whit I'm gonnae dae when I grow up?'

'Naw.'

'Well I'm gonnae be a fucking famous artist like Salvador Dali and I'm gonnae be in charge of that Art Gallery and I'm gonnae go right up tae that bastit and I'm gonnae go, hey Jimmy, eff off, you're oot, get lost. And he'll say whit for, whit's the game? And I'll say cause you're a stupit bastit and you don't know nothing aboot art, so just fuck off. Then know whit I'm gonnae dae?'

'Whit?'

'I'm gonnae take that picture aff the wa and I'm gonnae take it hame and I'm gonnae put it in the room just above the mantlepiece and I'm gonnae look and look and look.'

'Whit, that Three Graces?'

'Aye.'

'Christ, you really fancy that photie, don't you?'

'Dead right. I love that Rubens.'

Blush

Whenever Mina Sandison started thinking her house had reached the outermost limit of newfangledness; whenever she looked around at her television and her white sink unit and her white sideboard with the built-in secret drinks cabinet and her sliding glass door and her phone and her Venetian blinds and her stereophonic radiogram and her dimmable wall-lights; whenever she suspected that between her good taste and Tony's money they'd managed to get every single thing, then Tony, God bless him, would come singing through the door with something new. She cursed him often enough, and as often as not she shut him out on the landing or left him lying with a bleeding scalp while she carted herself and the kids off to her mother's for good. He was a devil, and young Tony was getting just as bad, and between the two of them they nearly drove her and Louise demented. But that was them, Big Tony and Wee Tony, Rogues Incorporated. She always brought them back from her mother's.

They pretended it was the conscience-presents he gave her that did the trick, but they both knew fine underneath it was nothing much to do with hair-dryers and dresses and gold bracelets, it was just Tony, Tony, Tony, him and his big blue eyes and his daft singing.

And nadjums.

She blushed in the empty room and looked around to make sure she was alone. The word, Tony's word, had slipped out, a detached link from her long happy chain of thought. She had never uttered it aloud before, and she always blushed when he used it, mostly because he said it with that look in his eye.

She had never had another man, never even seriously kissed anybody else, but she knew she was lucky to have got Tony. She knew it from the other women, how they looked and how they talked. Not that they ever said anything straight out, of course, but she knew from their voices and their eyes that they never went with their men where she went with her Tony. It was just part of the job for them, like cooking the dinner or washing the stairs – they got their thrills from the pictures or the True Romance stories. But she was the opposite; she wouldn't have traded Tony for a lorryload of Valentinos or Cary Grants, because he was her True Romance. The other women acted as if they were sorry for her because he was such a boozer and gambler and philanderer, but she knew they were jealous to their backteeth, and they would sell their sons to slavery for a chance to swop him with their own boring wee men even for one night. They did not understand: they thought she was the same as them, but if they'd only taken the trouble they could have seen right away she was different.

Her house was different and her children were different and she was dressed different and looked different. She looked younger, for a start – she was the same age, near enough, as Aggie Reid, but you might have thought there was twenty years between them. And Tony, my God, Tony was different. That wasn't snobbiness, that was just the truth. She got mad – screaming, raging, plate-smashing mad – but that was just part of being different. And what amazed her most was the things that got her angriest, the things she really wanted to kill him for – those were the very things that made her daft about him.

Especially his women. When she imagined Tony rolling about naked with Skinny Lucy or Madge Robertson or any of the rest it drove her nearly demented with jealousy, but it made her horribly excited as well. He knew that fine, and played on it. Sometimes on Friday nights he would bring in special drinks, liqueurs and things, and fancy chocolates, and make sure the kids were sleeping, and dim the wall-lights and really put on the Valentino act, feeding her just enough drink to make her soft and saying things she was sure none of the other women had even heard the likes of, except maybe Margot Connolly and Big Jessie. And it would start with her needing to be reassured she was his one and only girl and none of the others were worth a bean beside her, and that would mean talking about them, and even hearing their names would get her worked up as long as he kept hugging her and telling her she was the best, she was the best a mile. And that would work her up even further and she would start asking things and he would tease her into asking more and more and hug her tighter and she would get so excited she would shout the house down and feel things she knew none of the other women ever felt, except maybe Margot Connolly.

He was a devil, a pure devil, and Wee Tony was exactly the same – the other boys were jealous of him because he always had new things, things they'd never even heard of, and the girls gave him the glad-eye already, even though he was only eight.

New things. She looked around again and wondered if there could ever again be anything new, and the bell rang. It played the opening notes of 'Though April Showers May Come Your Way', and she could hear him singing along with it on the other side of the door.

She opened it and he poured in and kissed her and swung her on to the couch and planted a small suitcase-thing on the cushion beside her.

'What the hell's that?' she said, acting annoyed but laughing underneath.

'Magic, baby, magic.' He flicked open the two little clasps and lifted the lid.

'My god,' she said, 'it's one of them whatdyecallit things, the man on the TV had one – you can record yourself talking.'

'That's dead right, honeybaby, just wait till you hear this!'

He unwound the flex and leaned across the arm of the couch to plug the machine into the wall-socket. Young Tony and Louise, who had been playing up on the third landing, had heard their father's arrival, and came in hoping for chocolate. They had their own doorkey, a privilege he was never vouchsafed. Louise looked at the strange contraption with lady-like alarm, young Tony with excited curiosity.

'Got it off a fellow in the pub,' Big Tony said, as he threaded the tape into the reel. 'Fifteen quid the lot, tape thrown in. He's put a special long flex on the microphone, see? That's so's you can record things anywhere in the room, even if you've only the one socket. Great, eh?'

The women were doubtful, but young Tony was bouncing on his toes with eagerness.

'These women don't get the picture yet, son, but they soon will. Right then – just you wait, babies, you ain't seen nothing yet!'

He set the reels turning and picked up the microphone and was instantly, expertly, singing 'Nothing Could Be Finer Than To Be In Carolina In The Mo-o-o-rning' in a perfect Jolsonian parody. He stopped the tape and rewound it. Then, pausing dramatically with his finger over the PLAY button, he said, 'Now just you listen to this.'

He pressed the button and the room was filled again with Jolson, and even the women were impressed.

'Jesus Christ, that's great!' young Tony said. Mina

slapped his wrist lightly. 'Just you watch your language, my boy,' she said. 'You're not your daft father, you know.'

Louise tutted her support.

'Leave the boy alone,' said Tony. 'It's not every day you get something like this, is it?' He held the microphone out to Mina and said, 'Right then, you have a shot.'

'What? Not on your life!'

'Come on, don't be stupid, it's a laugh.'

'I can't sing, but.'

'You don't have to sing, just say something. You'll get a laugh, your voice sounds different when you hear it – everybody else knows it is you, but you don't.'

They were quiet then, and she eyed the microphone as she might have done a ferret poised at her throat.

'I can't think of anything to say,' she said, and blushed to her hair-roots.

Young Tony was feverish. 'My mammy's got a big riddy, a big riddy!' he shouted.

Louise pulled his arm. 'Tony she's *blushing*, you mean – talk properly.'

'Big riddy, big riddy!' he shouted again, defying his sister, pointing at his mother's crimson cheeks.

'That's enough, you, Cornflakes Kid, just you shut your mouth, not everybody's as gallus as you, thank Christ,' said Big Tony, and young Tony, who always did what his father told him, was quiet.

Finally Mina was induced to say 'Hullo, how you getting on?' and Louise recited 'Little Boy Blue' and young Tony did a passable parody of his father's parody of Jolson, and the women nearly died of embarrassment when they heard themselves rendered strange and unrecognizable through the machine.

Mina, thinking of the fifteen pounds, wondered what use the thing was really, and Tony expanded on the possibilities.

'Look, you know your favourite songs, like Jo Stafford and that? Well this tape lasts for an hour, so you play them on the radiogram and record them on to this, then you've got a whole hour of your favourites, non-stop – just press the button and you're away.'

She was almost convinced by that, but it was clear that a schism was developing between the female half of the family, which was becoming bored, and the male, which was warming to the limitless potential of the new wonder. Mina announced that she would have to go out to the butcher's to get something for the tea, and Louise said she would go with her.

'Right then, me and the Cornflakes Kid here will soon show you what use this thing is – we'll fix up a show you'll never forget, won't we son?'

'Dead right we will, Da,' said young Tony.

And when they came back Big Tony was standing beside the fireplace facing the door and young Tony was not to be seen; but the curtain of the kitchen recess was portentously drawn.

'Stop right there,' said Big Tony, raising his hand.

Then he turned to the curtain and said, 'Play maestro,' and the room filled with Big Band, and the intro finished and he was Crosby, crooning to them, dreamy-eyed and easy, oozing romance with 'Where the Blue of the Night Meets the Gold of the Day.'

'You're a daft messin, you really are,' said Mina, in a rare outburst of doting coarseness.

The music stopped with a small click from the recess, then he was Sinatra having 'One More for the Road', then Perry Como and Mario Lanza and Guy Mitchell and finally, ludicrously, so that even Louise rocked with laughter, Gracie Fields splitting her tonsils over 'Sally'.

It was a good week for Mina and Tony, and the mirth over

the tape-recorder was not a cause, but a mere symptom of it. Father Coming Home Drunk had never been a terrifying prospect for the Sandison children, because Tony, for all his reckless air, was careful about his limits, too much aware that his considerable social success lay in his twinkling eyes and quick tongue to let himself lose control of them. 'He's a bit stupit when he's got a drink in him.' This pronouncement, applied to some of the men, embraced a multitude of sins, from throwing money at children to savagely beating their wives; applied to Tony, as it often was, it was merely true.

Young Tony and Louise would lie on their plush new divan behind the sliding glass door, listening. If they heard just the doorbell and a morose silence, they knew he was sober and depressed about his health or his horses. If they heard the words of 'April Showers' accompanying the chime, they would giggle and Louise would give an old-fashioned tut-tut and young Tony would say, 'My da's steaming again,' and they would pretend to sleep but listen hard for his Jolson repertoire, muffled through the thick glass, and for their mother's laughter.

On Friday afternoon Tony took Mina into town to buy her a new watch because she had scratched the glass on the one he had given her for her birthday, and while they were away, young Tony had an idea. He demonstrated to a trembling Louise how it would work: with the machine safely tucked away in the corner of their bedroom, he could trail the long microphone-flex through the sliding door, along a yard of wall-skirting, to a perfect resting place behind the coach. By tucking the flex under the edge of the carpets, he could render the entire operation invisible.

'See,' he told her, giggling. 'When my da comes in the night steaming, I'll switch this on, then it'll record aw his songs and his stupit patter and my mammy laughing and we'll play it later and it'll be a rerr laugh.'

'Do you think so?' she asked, dubiously. 'Maybe they'll be annoyed.'

'Naw, whit is there to be annoyed aboot? My da'll love it.'

'OK,' she said, not entirely convinced, but swung by his air of confidence, and impressed by his cleverness.

He came in that night singing and happy, but very late, and when he checked in the bedroom he found two sincerely sleeping children. Flushed with a happy week and a happy evening, he sang a chorus of 'Mammy' then reached into his coat pocket and brought out a green bottle.

'Now, babydoll, just have a sook at this,' he said, waving it in front of her face.

'My God, what on earth is it?'

'Champagne, sweetheart, cham-fucking-pagne, the very best for the best wee doll in the world. Get a couple of glasses.'

He popped it open and held it up so the foam ran into his mouth, down his chin, over his shirt.

'Oh, so it's champagne is it? You never got that in The Wee Man. Where've you been then?' Her anger was half-real.

'Around, baby, around. Just you try some of this, then I'll show you the way to the stars.' He threw his coat off while she sat on the couch and sipped.

'It tastes like cider,' she said, wrinkling her nose.

'Cider at thirty-bob a bottle? Who do you think you're kidding? Throw that down and have another one.'

He tilted her glass, forcing her to swallow the wine, then topped her up again.

'You haven't told me where you've been – you're quite late tonight.' She could feel it again, rising from her stomach, that excitement that was almost a sickness, that desire that was almost disgust, and he saw it in her, and they both knew they were on the knife-edge, that his next few moves would determine whether it was to be a night of tears or of delight.

He kissed her, hard and full on the mouth, taking the glass from her hand so she was free to put her arms around him, and eased her down on to the cushions.

'You've been with that Skinny Lucy, again – I can always tell,' she said when he released her mouth.

'Baby, baby.' He kissed her brow, her eyelids, her ears. 'Never you mind where I've been, it's where I'm going that matters.'

'Oh you're a right swine – that's what you're so happy about, you've been with her, you've been with that dirty whore.'

He kissed her again, gentle with his lips this time, but more insistent with his hands, pressing her, stroking, forcing her to relax, to respond. And when he felt he was winning, he let her go and handed her back her glass. She took one sip, and when she opened her mouth to speak, he placed another soft kiss on her lips, claiming the initiative. With his tongue he teased her into opening her mouth for him and as she did so, hardly aware of what she was doing, she began to undo the buttons of her dressing-gown.

'You're the only one for me, babydoll, it's you I get my nadjums from,' he whispered in her ear.

'Me and twenty-three others.'

'You're the best, you're the only one that's worth a bean.'

This, for her, was the dreaded moment, when she could start the perilous journey that would see her tortured with jealousy and rage and drive her wild with delight. She remembered Arthur, her daft brother, sitting her in his soapbox cart at the top of the Glenfield Street Hill and placing her hand on the brake-lever that was the only thing between safety and a mad career down to the Road and daring her to release it, and how she shook and how her hand froze to the lever. She took a large swallow of champagne.

'Am I really?'

'Really really really,' he said putting his arms around her inside the dressing-gown, against the silk of her nightdress.

'Better than that Doris Carter?'

'A million mile.'

'Better than that Jessie Anderson?'

'No bother.'

'Better than that Skinny Lucy?'

'Baby, she's nothing to you, she's just a bag of mutton-bones.'

'Yes, but you like her.'

'A bit.'

'A big bit.'

'No, a wee bit.'

'What wee bit? What do you like best about her? What do you do with her?'

'Not half as much as I do with you, baby.'

'Oh but come on, tell me, tell me what you do, tell me what she likes.'

She had released the brake now: the jealousy and the fear and the rage beat at her ribs, more powerful than ever, but they merged with a churning in her stomach and a trembling in the backs of her legs, merged into a single whelming delight, and when he eased her down to the cushions again and said, 'She likes this!' she squealed, a high witless happy squeal such as none of the other women ever made, except maybe Big Jessie and Margot Connolly.

It penetrated the sliding glass door, that squeal, and found young Tony stirring from his sleep and fuzzily recollecting his great idea.

'Louise,' he whispered, but he heard only the deep breathing of blissful unconsciousness.

He lay for a moment peering through the glass at the dimmed light of the living-room, hearing the muffled noises of his parents romp on the couch, re-establishing his contact with the waking world. Then he remembered.

There was enough light from the other room and from the street to make the task easy. He slipped out of bed, not knowing how utterly secure he was from detection by the occupants of the couch next door. The RECORD button was larger than the others, and easy to find. He pressed it, then crept back into bed and unperturbed at having missed the prelude to the night's entertainment and safely assured that he could listen to the main performance at his leisure, he fell asleep.

When they rose on the Saturday morning, Tony had the appetite of a man simply pleased with himself, and Mina was quiet with a contentment, as always only a little guilt-tinged. They were a full hour later in stirring than the children, and it was noon by the time they finished breakfast, time for Tony to be winding up for his Saturday revels.

He proposed a trip to Dumbrusco's.

'Come on we'll buy in some drink and I'll bring some of the company up here from the pub tonight. It's been about fifty year since we had a wee do here.'

'Och, do you think we should?' It was a token protest: Mina never visited the pub herself, but she had no real objection to admitting some of its denizens into her Hollywood home occasionally, where they could see her as the stately hostess and where she could reaffirm her superiority – her difference.

He coaxed her and kissed her nose and finally she said, 'All right, but not too many, and don't bring that Pat

MacKay, he stubs out his cigarettes on the furniture, and that Jock Simpson, he's always fighting.'

So they left, and young Tony, who had cleared up the evidence while they slept but had not dared to listen to the results of his cleverness, wound the tape back to the beginning, beckoned Louise to kneel down beside him and with a trembling finger pushed the PLAY button. There was a slight hiss of neutral tape, then a click, then the bedroom was filled with Crosby-crooning.

'Shit!' he said and stood up and stamped.

'Tony, watch your language,' said his sister.

'But Christ, it hasnae worked.'

'You must have done something wrong in the dark.'

'Naw I didnae. Look, there's the button there – it's easy tae see, it's bigger than the other waans. Oh fuck it!'

'Tony! You'll go to the Bad Place!'

He was kneeling again, ignoring her rebuke, pushing buttons, stopping the tape then running it forwards at speed. He pushed PLAY and they heard the final flourish of 'Where the Blue of the Night', then a click, then, unmistakably, the high and almost hysterical tones of a woman, their mother, laughing.

'That's it!' he cried in triumph, and at the same moment they heard the key turning in the door. He stopped the tape and stood up. 'It wasnae at the start o the tape when I pressed the button – it starts eftir the Bing Crosby song – stoating!' he whispered.

'What are you two up to then?' his father asked, dropping two Mars Bars on to the table. He was twinkling all over. 'Hope you've not been messing about with that tape-recorder.'

'Naw, Da, we havenae touched it,' said young Tony, brazenly, while Louise turned away to hide her blush.

It was a biggish Saturday-night gathering – most of the

regulars and a few strays in addition – that followed Tony home on the promise of screw-tops and Johnnie Walker and other, more mysterious, delights. Pat MacKay had been safely avoided, but Jock Simpson had insinuated his way into the company, and Tony was too happy to object.

Tam Burke was dropped into his usual place in the big armchair, and sat with his banjo across the place where his legs should have been, modestly deferring to his host's known musical talents by waiting till he was asked before he would play. The rest draped themselves comfortably over the chairs and table and sideboard and held out their hands for glasses, and Big Jessie sat on the couch commenting on how much the place had changed since she lived in it.

When he had furnished everybody with a drink Tony whispered in Mina's ear, and she protested.

'No, no, I don't know what you're thinking of – it's too late for a wean to be up, and anyway, I don't want him among all this.'

'It'll just be five minutes, honest baby, and he'll be in the recess there, out of the road. Please, honeydoll, just for me – he won't be sleeping anyway.'

'No, and that's final.'

'Honeybabe!'

'No, Tony.'

He put his lips to her ear and whispered in his Cary Grant voice the words he had used the night before: 'Only you, darling, only you – you're the best, the best, the best.'

'Oh God,' she said, shuddering and blushing to her ears, 'OK, but only if he's awake.'

He was. Tony lifted him from the bed and carried him across the jungle of legs to the curtain of the recess. Busy with their drinks, and continuing now their argument and raillery from the pub, the guests took no notice. Tony stood young Tony beside the curtain and whispered to him, 'Listen, son. I've wound the tape back to the start, so just you slip in there and do exactly what you did the other day, right? When I say "Take it away, maestro."'

'But Da, I don't want tae,' said young Tony, looking around at the revellers and beginning to panic. 'I'm feart.'

'Feart? There's nothing to be feart about. Come on, just for five minutes, just to please your daft old da – please?'

He was already pushing young Tony through the curtain. 'Always does what his daddy tells him, that boy. He's a wee smasher,' he said to the recumbent Bumpstead Ruskin, who had been eavesdropping on the last part of the conversation. Bumpstead shrugged and took a slug from his screwtop.

Tony coughed and moved to the middle of the floor and lifted his hands in a signal that they all understood.

'Best of order now, ladies and gentlemen, best of order. What do you say it's time for a song?'

They said loudly that it was.

'Right then, what'll it be – bit of the old banjo from our Tam here?'

Tam, as Tony knew he would, shook his head.

'Naw, naw,' he said. 'The host first. How's about a bit of Jolson fae you, Tony?' And they took up the cry, with requests for 'Swannie River', 'Mammy', 'Robert E. Lee', till he silenced them again.

'No,' he said. 'We'll give that Jolson a rest, bugger that Jolson. Tell you what – we'll have a bit of the old Bing Crosby, OK?'

They were puzzled, but sensing something in the air, agreed. He picked up the microphone, snapped his fingers, and called to the curtain, 'Take it away, maestro.'

The band played, at first to an amazed silence, then, when they saw the game, to roars of laughter, and he crooned them through 'Where the Blue of the Night' and they joined in raucously and with growing hysteria to the flourishes. Then the music stopped and there were cheers and stampings and calls for more.

'Don't worry, folks,' said Tony in his best American accent, 'you ain't heard nothin yet. How's about a bit of Frankie Sinatra?'

Sinatra suited them fine, and he snapped his fingers again and said, 'Take it away, maestro.' Nothing happened, and he laughed and pulled the curtain aside and said in a whisper full of mock-menace, 'Take it AWAY, maestro!'

And young Tony, 'who always did what his daddy told him', pushed the PLAY button.

They called it a great night, a really great night – that night when that stuck-up Mina Sandison and that gallus Tony Sandison got a big riddy.

Granny Sloag's Secret

Mother-in-laws? Mother-in-laws? Don't talk to me aboot them, Christ. Nae wunner they've got aw they jokes, nae wunner that bampot Tony Sandison sings that stupit song – whit is it again? – I love my mother-in-law, I'd love to break her jaw. Break her jaw, that's a laugh – I'd break her bloody neck forby, and that's nae kidding, that's the God honest truth.

I know it's no her fault, really. I blame him for it, even although he's deid. He made her life a misery. Fair enough, he worked hard an that, did aw they late shifts, but, Christ, the way he sat in that chair, like a bloody great elephant, shouting at her. 'Netta,' he used tae shout, 'Netta, you've no stirred this.' And she'd go running for a spoon and come through and stir his tea for him, honest tae God, an aw the thanks she ever got was a dirty look. Nae wunner she took tae the bottle, you can hardly blame her, the life she had.

The two lassies were quite a good help tae her, mind. My Peggy was aye a good worker, even when she was at the school, and Mary's just a wee stoater, she does aw her messages and her cleaning still. She's up the same close, like. But Sandy, he's a chancer, a real chanty-wrastler: he treats his wife same as the auld yin treated his ma – just a bloody slave.

I'm no a drinker, myself. That whisky turns my stomach, and I don't know how they can drink that beer. A half at the New Year's my limit, and even then I have tae force it doon. Mind you, I didnae have tae force it doon this New Year, ha, ha – but that's whit my story's aboot, you'll have tae wait a bit for that.

Funny thing is, they never had drink in their hoose – never a drap. And he hardly ever went tae the pub, just noo and again on his way back fae work, and aw she ever got was a sherry sometimes on a Saturday if he took her tae the lounge, and her wee hauf on New Year's Day. They werenae whit you'd call drinkers, nane of the two of them, no even at Hogmanay, that's how it was funny when she started on it, that's how naebody would believe him at first.

She should never've gied up her work, that was the really stupit thing, she had a rerr wee job in McCann's office, she didnae have tae chuck that just cause she was sixty, Christ, he'd've kept her on as long as she liked, he knew he was on a good thing. Waance the family was up and merried she just got bored, she just didnae seem tae have anything left tae live for. Then he got that heart trouble, that angina, and he went semi-retired and did his part-time watchman at the whisky-bond. So that was just him and her, just the two of them, sitting staring at each other, and they'd never really had much interest in life ootside their works and their family, so he just put on the weight – Christ, he went like an elephant, so he did – and she got bored.

Still an aw, we got a shock when drink first got mentioned. I first got the wire fae my Peggy. 'My da thinks my ma's been on the drink,' says she when she comes back fae visiting them waan night. I nearly jumped oot my shirt. 'She's whit?' I said. I couldnae believe my ears. 'He thinks she's drinking behind his back,' says she. 'When he's oot at the bond. He says he comes hame and she's talking funny – slurring her words.' That was the first I heard aboot it, Christ, it wasnae the last.

'Christ Peg,' says I, 'she's an auld woman, everybody talks funny when they get aulder.'

'She's no that auld, she's only sixty-three. Anyway, he says she's staggering, sometimes, fawing aboot the flerr and that.'

'Staggering my arse. It's him that's staggering, merr liker. He's gaun mental, so he is.' I was on her side, I couldnae believe that aboot her.

'Maybe, maybe no,' says my Peggy. 'We've tae smell her breath.'

'Smell her breath. Whit the fuck for?'

'He cannae smell, he never could. He says we've tae smell her breath and tell him if she's been at the wine.'

'Jesus Christ, that's gonnae look great, i'n't it? Sticking wir noses in her mooth every time she breathes.'

But that's whit we done, nae kidding. Imagine it – her sitting in her chair blethering and us aw leaning ower sniffing like dugs. You felt a right mug, I never seen anything so stupit in my life. And you could never tell anyway – she was too fly, they're always too fly, they alcoholics. She used to eat they Clarnico Mint Creams aw the time, that was aw the smell you ever got, that bloddy peppermint, and I don't even like it, Christ. She must've ate boxes of the things.

And them two middle waans of Mary's – that Ellen and that Margaret, them wi the fancy boyfriends, Christ, talk aboot stuck-up, talk aboot snobs! Whit a pair a fancy-drawers – they're gaun aboot saying 'Ooh, I do hope Gran isn't taking to drink at her time of life, it would be such a pity, she's always been so good.'

Fucking dead right she's been good. She's a lot better woman than they'll ever be, for aw their fancy boyfriends and their spiced steak fae the butcher's at two-an-nine a pun. Funny they should've turnt oot like that, a right couple of snobs – young Ena's the opposite, she's just like Mary, she's a good plain lassie, she'd gie ye the shirt off her back; and young Mary, the youngest lassie, she's a wee smasher, she's my favourite of the lot; and the boys are OK, my Peggy's been like another mother tae them, so she has – we never had any of wir ain, funny enough.

Anyway, that smelling her breath was a dead loss, we just felt stupit, then waan eftirnoon he comes up the stair tae Mary's – she was just clearing away the dishes and my Peggy was there helping her, and he come busting in and he's got this bottle in his haun, an empty hauf-bottle of VP, and he hauds it up and says: 'There yous are, yous wantit proof – there it fucking is.'

'Where'd that come fae?' they said.

'Her bag, I fun it in her handbag,' says he.

Well that looked like proof right enough, so they baith went doon wi him tae the first landing tae face her wi it, like, and Christ, she just sits there and draws her heid back and says:

'It's a lie. He's a bloody auld liar. He put that bottle in my bag, he planted it. May God strike me doon deid if I tell a lie – I've never seen that bottle in my life before.'

So they never knew whit tae think. He looked as if he wantit tae strangle her on the spot, but she just sat there and brass-necked it. See, you don't know her, she was aye such a plain sort of woman, awful sort of dignified, you couldnae imagine her telling a lie, like. So Peggy and Mary didnae know whit tae think, and he was gaun up the pole, the auld bugger. It was me, later on, when Peggy was telling me aboot it, it was me that said:

'Whit the hell would she want tae plank an empty bottle fur? It's a full waan she would've had planked in her bag,' and Peggy said 'Right enough, she's no that stupit.'

Be that as it may, he started hitting her eftir that. Nothing you could prove for definite, like, but he usetae come in fae that bond and accuse her of being drunk and there'd be a right barney and he'd belt her aboot. Waance she had a cracked rib – supposed tae a fell against the sideboard for that. Then she'd a lump on her heid the size of a duck's egg – that was the door of the kitchen cabinet, so he said. Gie her her due, she never accused him, and she'd never've shopped him tae the polis or that, but you could tell it in his face he was guilty.

So it got tae be pure murder and you couldnae tell who was the worser bampot, him or her, and it got so's you hated gaun up tae see them cause you never knew whit you'd find, and it was a relief really – I hate tae say that but it's true – it was a relief when he took a bad turn wi his heart waan Friday and they took him intae the Royal and he died on the Sunday night.

Eftir that it didnae seem tae matter even if she was taking a wee drap on the fly – she wasnae daeing any herm, was she? And Mary and her family were there tae keep an eye on her, and we were just up 14, just a couple of closes away. No that you wanted her tae go ower the score, like. I mean waance or twice she tapped the neighbours for money and Mary and Peggy had to pay them back and tell them tae stop lending her it. And that stupit Lily McCaffrey, she usetae encourage her, she usetae gie her the stuff, stupit bitch, she wants shooting.

The laugh was, naebody ever talked aboot it, or admitted it. If anybody offered her a drink she aye refused, she just sat there wi her back straight and her heid up and said, 'No thanks, I never touch it.' And some of the family, like that stupit pair of bitches, that Ellen and Margaret, they still never believed it.

So it was a secret. Whit a bloody laugh, the worst kept secret in Scotland – the whole stair knew aboot it except some of her ain family. Whit she did was, she'd listen at the door for some wean tae come past – usually it was waan of they wee Ruskins fae next door – and she'd open the door and catch them and say: 'Here's a wee threepenny bit for you, could you just take this haufcroon doon tae

Dumbrusco's and ask him for a wee bottle of South African sherry – just tell him it's for your mammy, tell him she's making trifles.' Christ, auld Dumbrusco must've thought the whole building was trifle-daft.

Anyway, then comes the New Year, then comes the real laugh.

Even eftir he was deid a year or two we still kept up the family tradition: Peggy and me and Mary and Wullie and their family would aw go tae her hoose and firstfit her on New Year's Day, before dinner-time, just for the waan drink, like. It was the only time in the year I ever spoke tae Wullie Moore, he's an awful nice man, Wullie, but he just stays in that bed of his aw the time and you never see him; and it was the only drink I ever touched, just tae bring the New Year in, and I had tae force it doon. So this guy at work, he'd got a haud of these crates of Black and White just afore Christmas, and he was selling it for eleven-bob a bottle – still too fucking dear, if you ask me, but it was a good bargain, so I took two aff him. Then I goes up tae Granny Sloag's the day efter Christmas and I says, 'Here Maw, I've brought you the New Year bottle for when the family comes, right?' And I opens the kitchen cabinet and sticks it right in at the back – she'd've needed a chair tae get tae it – and I says, 'Noo listen, Maw, I'm putting this in here and you've no tae touch it tae New Year's Day, it's for the family – OK?'

'Right you are, Tommy, you're a good son-in-law tae me. I won't touch it.'

'You promise?' says I.

'Cross my heart, son, I'll no even look at it.'

See, I could always talk straight wi her, and she was always straight wi me, she never tried tae kid me like she did the rest of them.

So we were in and oot a few times that week and we kept taking a fly look in the cabinet just tae check she hadnae been at the bottle and sure enough it was just sitting there, exactly where I left it, and full tae the tap.

Hauf-eleven on New Year's morning. Whit a collection: Wullie Moore was in his good suit, it was bad enough seeing him in daylight, but wearing his good suit – he was like something fae another planet so he was, something fae Mars. And I was wearing a collar and tie and Peggy and Mary were in the good frocks and the four lassies were aw dolled up. Ellen's boyfriend, he was waan of they American sailors, and he was in his uniform and you could see she thought she was the bee's knees sitting there wi a Yank, hingin on his erm. And Margaret was even worse, Christ: she won a competition at Butlin's waance and ever since she's thought she was a filmstar – Doris Day or somebody. I waance said tae Peggy, 'Doris Day? Doris Day? – She looks like Boris Karloff tae me,' but that wasnae right, she's a good looking girl, I must admit. Her boyfriend was waan of they solicitors or something, and he was sitting there in his pinstrip suit wi a waistcoat and a gold chain and everything. And the two boys were there as well, aw done up in their Sunday best. So we moved the table and put aw the chairs in a big circle roon the fire and Granny had already got the bottle oot and I gied everybody a gless. The women got they wee toatie waans, like thimbles, wi kilties on them playing the bagpipes, and the men got big tumblers. Then she lifts the bottle tae pour the drinks and the big solicitor-guy stauns up and says, 'Hang on, Mrs Sloag, just you sit down and I'll do that for you.' She already had the tap aff, and she hauns the bottle tae him and he guides her doon tae the big ermchair and sits her doon. I thought the bastit was being a bit forward, mysel, but I looked across at Margaret and she was twirling her big engagement ring and looking at the big bastit like he was Superman or something.

He goes roon the circle and he pours us aw a drink and

when he gets back tae his ain chair there's just enough left for a good-sized hauf, so he empties it intae his gless and sits doon and says, 'Very neat, eh?' And Margaret looks up intae his eyes like he was Jesus Christ, stupit bitch.

So there we're aw sitting, staring at each other, wondering whit the hell happens next. The boys have got their drink as well – that raspberry cordial stuff that nips your throat. And we're beginning tae feel stupit, sitting there like dummies, and Mary pokes Wullie wi her elbow and he clears his throat and hauds oot his gless and says, 'Well here's tae us aw, and I hope we aw have a happy New Year.'

I could see Ellen and Margaret looking at each other and moving their eyebrows, thon way, then Wullie slugs his drink doon in a waanie, dead embarrassed, and bows his heid doon, and the rest of us say Happy New Year and sip wir drinks. Peggy, she just kids on she's drinking it as usual – she cannae stand the stuff, same as me, she really never touches it. Noo I'm no a whisky drinker, like I said already, it makes me sick – but this stuff, soon as I tasted it I said tae mysel, oh-ho, there's something no right here, this is no the roon shilling, this. I looked across at the rest of the company – young Mary and Ena and Ellen and Margaret and their smart-arse boyfriends – and I could see them aw looking really funny, really embarrassed like. So I took another wee sip, and that proved it. I leaned ower tae Peggy and whispered in her ear.

'Peggy?'

'What?'

'Have you tasted that?'

'Naw, you know I never touch it.'

'Well taste it.'

'What for?'

'Just taste it, will you?'

The rest of them were beginning tae talk among

theirsels, so we could talk OK withoot being noticed, like. She took a wee toatie sip.

'Whit aboot it?' she whispered tae me.

'Taste it again.'

She was getting a bit mad wi me, but she lifted her gless again and while she was sipping it I said, 'It's watter, pure watter.'

'Jesus,' she said, 'so it is.'

She looked roon at the rest of them.

'The fly auld bitch,' I said, 'that was good whisky. She's been drinking it aw week and wattering it doon.'

'I thought it looked a bit white,' she said.

'Aye, she's been putting tea in, but no enough.'

'Don't say anything,' Peggy whispered.

'Whit. Are we just tae sit here like a bunch of nutters, sooking watter?'

'Aye.'

'OK. Suits me fine, I hate the stuff anyway. But I wonder whit these guys are thinking.'

I could feel Peggy shaking when I said that, she was nearly busting oot laughing so she was.

So we aw sat there in a circle, sipping watter and talking, and then auld Granny butts in really loud and says, 'This is lovely, it's lovely having aw my family roon me at the New Year, it's that good of you aw tae come, it really is.'

And she sits there aw straight and serious, and a wee tear comes creeping doon her cheek oot her left eye, and I looked at her and thought tae mysel you fly auld bisum, I wonder whit you're really thinking there, I bet you're laughing yourself stupit inside, sitting there like the Queen of Sheba watching us mugs bringing the New Year in wi pure bloody watter.

Limpy Dan

I know I'll never make sergeant, I know that fine. In fact, with my temper I'm lucky I've kept the job this long. Not that it's much of a job these days. My God, there's no respect these days, I was better off in the army. McGuire says most of the complaints he gets in the office are about me. That's an exaggeration, but I take his point, as long as he takes mine. I've got the bum steer, so I'm bound to get more of the trouble. That No. 30 and that No. 14, the sooner they demolish that lot the better. They've been condemned for years, but they just sit there.

I can't keep my temper, I just explode, I mean, how would you feel? There you are doing your best for them, you're knocking your pan in trying to make life a bit decenter, trying to stop the gambling and the thieving and the razor-slashing, and what thanks do you get?

Limpy Dan the funny big man. Even the weans shout abuse at me, and the old ones encourage them. Limpy Dan the funny big man. What kind of attitude is that? Where's the respect? A lot of the bigger ones are in the army now, thank God, but the younger ones are growing up even worse.

Gambling? Don't talk to me about gambling. It's every house the same – the old ones in the kitchen playing solo, the young ones ben the room playing haepenny brag. If it's not that it's pitch-and-toss in the backcourt and that Barney the Book shuffling from corner to corner to give me the slip. God knows, I'm not your lily-white plaster saint, I don't mind the odd punt, but with this lot it's punt

punt punt, they'd stake their granny's false teeth, so they would.

They hate my guts because I don't let them relax. I make their life a misery, but my God, it's not easy. Corroboration – I could swing for that bloody corroboration. I've told young Blake, wherever he is, whatever he's seen or not seen, he corroborates me and I corroborate him, tit for tat. He was a bit chary at first but I told him that this was a war against crime and it was stupid for them to have real bullets and us to have blanks and he took my point. In fact, he's even keener than me now. The other night he handcuffed a bloke to a shop door and came for me and I went and corroborated for him. He'll be a sergeant before I will, that boy.

I don't hate them – mostly I feel sorry for them – but I have to act hard for their own good, I have to put on the tough-guy act, the Broderick Crawfords. That's what usually brings in the complaints, that's what gets McGuire on to me telling me I'm too zealous in the performance of my duty. It's all right for him to talk, he doesn't have to deal with them, he doesn't have to take the abuse.

Like the other week I got threatened by that Phil Findlay and damn me if McGuire doesn't go greasing up to him, backing him against me. OK so Findlay had a point, I'll admit that, but that's no excuse for McGuire – your sergeant should back you to the hilt, rough or smooth, that's my opinion.

It was that boy of Findlay's, that Alastair, that caused it.

We had a plan, young Blake and me – we knew we could nab at least eight of them – boys from the school (I hate the summer holidays, I really hate them) and layabouts. They were playing pitch-and-toss in the back, in the space between 30 and 14, in behind the billboard. We worked out a pincer-movement, young Blake through 30 and me through 14, but that wee O'Hara, the snottery one whose a bit soft in the head, he spotted us from across the Road and was off his mark like a shot and up the billboard like a monkey warning them before I even reached the back-close. I thought we might still nab them, but damn me, they'd rigged up a ladder on the wash-house dyke and they were across to Kenny Street before we could get anywhere near them.

Jesus Christ, I was mad. Lucky for young O'Hara he was still up the billboard – I'd've throttled him soon as look at him. I shouted up at him, 'Right you, get across that billboard and down here, on the double, you've got some talking to do.'

I got him by the throat and shoved him up against the billboard and told young Blake to have the notebook handy. There was a crowd of the younger kids gathering round but I didn't mind that, I thought it might do them good to see the interrogation and we might get a few more names from them.

'OK, sonny boy,' I said, pinning him to the billboard. 'You'll get twenty years in the Bar-L for that, but if you talk I'll let you off ten of them.' His face was covered in green snotters and some went on my uniform and made me even wilder. I was nearly choking him, and he was howling blue murder, and some of the other kids were howling as well.

We got loads of names: four up 14 and five up 30, but the trouble was it was just any old names, he was that scared. Some of them were there, fair enough, but the rest! We got Alan Brass, who's in Catterick, we got Francie Kenny, who was in the Infirmary with an abscess, and we got young Findlay, the rat, who was away for an interview with the Merchant Navy. So when they all got their summonses there was pandemonium. Phil Findlay got off his work early and came up to the station just when I was coming off my shift. He's only five-foot-four,

Findlay, but he's built like Maxie Baer and he was a pretty good welter-weight before he put the beef on. He came right up to me and put his hand on my chest. I was a good head taller than him but I kept my temper because McGuire was watching every move.

'Right, McGlaughlin, you've bloody done it this time, you big dreep,' says Findlay.

I tried to be reasonable in front of McGuire. 'Listen Phil,' says I. 'There's been a wee misunderstanding, OK?'

'Don't you Phil me, you bloody chanty-wrastler, I'll put your head through that effing wall, polis or no polis,' says he. He was really blazing, and he's a strong wee bugger.

'I think it's time we all calmed down a bit, Mr Findlay,' says McGuire. 'The officer's made his apology, and you'll get an official letter in the post that clears your boy's name.'

'Bloody right I will. And just you tell that chanty-wrastler to leave off my Alastair. This is no the first time. My Christ, he got him last year for loitering and the boy was only waiting at the close for his sister to come oot the fish-shop. Fourteen bob that cost us, and it's cost the boy his place in the Merchant Navy, they're saying he's got a record, for Christ's sake – a record for seeing his sister hame fae the fish-shop!'

I don't know how I kept my temper, job or no job, but McGuire was still crawling. 'Oh, did he fail his interview?' says he. 'I'm sorry to hear that, Mr Findlay.'

'Sorry your arse,' says Findlay. 'It was that stumor (pointing at me) that caused it.'

He went to the door, but he still wasn't finished. He shouted back at McGuire while he was opening it.

'You tell him (me again) if he comes near my boy he'll be needing another wooden leg.'

The bastard. I really don't know how I kept my temper. They always say I've got a wooden leg just because I've got a slight limp. It was rickets caused that, when I was young.

Anyway, that's McGuire. That's the kind of rat that gets to be a sergeant.

Cowgirl

They were all surprised and nobody was fooled when Sawdust McGlashen and Coaldust McCann went in cahoots with the Corporation to build the Pensioners' Hall. They didn't have to ask if McGlashen would be supplying the timber to build it and McCann the coal to heat it.

'That bastit McGlashen, rich as Carnegie and wouldnae give ye a bag of sawdust, wouldnae give ye a stick to kennle your fire, neither he would.'

'Aye, and that McCann, his coal's nothing but bloody stanes, well seeing he's rolling in it.'

'Aye, and there's nane of the two of them would buy you a gless of water. Come into that pub like they owned it, drinking that Dimple and that Black Label. Bastits.'

'Aye, they think your heid's buttoned up the back, these people.'

'Bastits.'

The adults hated the Hall because it was new and the children, fairer, hated it because it cut off half the backcourt prairie and most of the thrilling length of the wash-house dyke, and because there was barbed wire on the eaves to stop them from climbing on to the corrugated iron roof. Not even the pensioners, the ostensible beneficiaries, had a good word for it, and Granny Sloag said she wouldn't be seen dead in it for all the tea in China.

But she was in the front row for the first Friday-night concert, and like everyone else, she pronounced it wonderful.

McGlashen was the impresario and the MC, and his programme was a cunning blend of local favourites and imported professional talent.

Tam Burke was the first turn – sitting in a cane chair with his empty trouser-legs dangling, taking them through 'The Cowboy's Wedding Day' and 'Broken Hearted Clown' and the rest of his repertoire. Then Tony Sandison came on covered in boot polish and did Jolson numbers and Barney the Book told jokes about Pat Mick and the Irishman and Elkie Jackson did Jimmy Shand on the accordion and the Boys' Brigade sang Boys' Brigade songs.

These familiar things softened them up for the second half, when the top-billed people appeared: the Smith Brothers wore kilts and sang Scotch favourites and The Great Ronaldi, who had taught Houdini everything he knew, escaped from a coalsack and a vast poundage of chains in less than ten seconds. The whole building shook when Annie MacGinty, the singing cowgirl, danced on, twirling ropes and stunning everyone in her white stetson and frilled buckskin shirt, and her sequinned short skirt and white boots, singing 'You Can't Get a Man with a Gun' in a gravelly voice that bypassed your ears and went straight to your ribs.

By the time she reached her final number – her trademark – 'Let Him Go, Let Him Tarry', the Hall was in dangerous uproar, and it was a piece of inspired improvization by McGlashen that brought forward the appearance of Barry O'Boyle, the Irish tenor. The women adored him so much they forced the men and the children to silence, and such was the change of atmosphere wrought by his rendition of 'Mother MacCree' that even some of the men were sniffling into their sleeves.

After the singing cowgirl, however, there had to be some sense of anti-climax. Ronnie Martino, who topped the bill, was shrewd enough to spot this, and knew he would have to pull out all the stops in his impersonations of Dickie Valentine impersonating other people. When he did his version of Valentine's version of Johnnie Ray's 'Gladrag Doll', he cried huge tears and stamped all over the stage and after he had torn his jacket to shreds a girl came on with another one and he put that on and ripped it to pieces as well. It was a masterly mix of pathos and comedy, and got the applause it deserved, but when Sawdust McGlashen stepped out to wish them all a safe walk home, the cries were for Annie MacGinty. He stuck out his rich wobbly belly and raised his hands for order, but their enthusiasm merged with their loathing of him into a menacing implacability.

It was, strangely, an over-the-score jibe from Pat MacKay, the most drunken and most vicious-tongued member of the audience, that restored the peace. He broke free from Rosie MacKay's restraining grasp, stood up and shouted:

'You get aff that stage, you fat bastit, we want the cowgirl!' This caused a ripple of indignation, not only because Pat was nearly as well-loathed as Sawdust himself, but because it jarred with the prevailing conviviality of the evening.

When McGlashen said, 'Now you're out of order there, my friend, you're way over the score,' he was gratifyingly supported, and Pat was made to sit down, mumbling that he only wanted the same as everybody else, and he didn't see what the bloody argument was about.

And, skilfully filling the embarrassed silence, Sawdust McGlashen made the announcement:

'Now, ladies and gentlemen, by special request, Scotland's answer to Annie Oakley, the one and only Annie MacGinty!' And her long blonde tresses bounced under the stetson and her buckskin frills danced as she rasped and her delirious audience roared through three more choruses of 'Let Him Go, Let Him Tarry'.

There were no spoil-sport voices as they spilled out into the night, still humming the chorus.

'That was marvellous, pure marvellous, so it was.'

'See that Annie MacGinty? She should be in the pictures, so she should.'

'Nae bother.'

'She's better'n that Betty Hutton a mile.'

'A mile? Christ two mile. That Betty Hutton couldnae hold a candle to her, neir she could.'

The Friday-night concerts became a once-a-month fixture, and Annie MacGinty went to the top of the bill and stayed there. Everybody was in love with her, and for the full week before each concert they hummed 'Let Him Go, Let Him Tarry' in happy unconscious anticipation.

Into the life of John Findlay she came as a worrying intrusion. He had been in love often enough before, but no previous attachment had seriously impinged upon his arrangement with Joan Reid, who lived straight above him in the first house, third landing, and had a paralysed right arm and whom he was pledged to marry.

Between them were just two days and a shared oddness. Bella Findlay, directly underneath, had heard big Aggie Reid being delivered of Joan those two days before she herself bore John, so the two women somehow, without saying a word on the matter, connived at and took pleasure in the growing affinity between the children. Not that there was ever any talk of them being sweethearts; at five John had gone to the Protestant school and Joan to the Catholic, and while he was blonde and twinkling and the best climber in the tenement, she was mousy and solemn and round-shouldered and from the age of two had had only one serviceable arm. It was their secret, solemnized across the years in ways that they were hardly aware of, in looks and chance remarks and rare touches of hands and, only once, officially and explicitly; at his sixth birthday party, she had sat on his bed in her shabby pink party-dress with her head bowed and her thin dead arm held by the wrist in her good left hand and had said 'OK' when he told her they would get married when they were about twenty-one even though she was two days older than him and it would have been better the other way round.

Even within her own family Joan was an odd thing. She had not entirely escaped the Reid squint – a legacy from both parents. But what in the rest of the family was a bizarre and, for strangers, alarming disfigurement, appeared in her as a mere hint of otherness that added to her general air of saintliness. In her, Big Aggie's buxom good looks and Tom Reid's wiry ugliness had merged, for the only time, felicitously. She was not as simply beautiful as John's cousin Louise whom he also loved and who was likewise touched with saintliness, but he knew that his relationship with Joan was altogether more serious. Excluded by her infirmity from their more boisterous games, she would sit on a window-sill and watch, and he felt her watching him and she knew that his most audacious leaps and most daring climbs were done to please her.

But by the third Friday-night concert, which he saw from the front row, he was desperately in love with the bright blonde vigour of the singing cowgirl and beginning, guiltily, to regret his promises to Joan. He was still flushed with the excitement of it when he changed into his pyjamas, and he marvelled that his father had been able to sit snoring by the radio in blissful insouciance while wonders had been transpiring practically next door.

'You really missed yourself the night, Da, it was great.'

'Aye? Was that wee Burke still banging his banjo?'

'Aye, he was OK. You know that Annie MacGinty?'

'What? Her with the hat? What aboot her?'
'Is she a real cowgirl?'
'What d'you mean?'
'Does she come fae America, like?'
'America? Well she's from the Wild West all right.'
'Whereaboots?'
'Talbot Street. Her auld man used to run that Jack of Diamonds pub. Peter MacGinty. I done some jobs for him couple of years back, mean auld bugger. He died last year with that whitdyecallit, that pleurisy.'

Talbot Street. The answer was not disappointing. Talbot Street was a mere four blocks away (westward, to be sure), but deep enough into that hinterland of tiled closes and stained-glass to seem exotic.

'She's great at they lasso-tricks.'
'Aye, she learnt that at the pub. It's full of bloody cowboys, that place.'

She lived at No. 28. He went there the following morning with a bundle of comics and found the house on the first storey. The brass nameplate said P. MACGINTY, and there was a brass doorknocker. He knocked and a grey-haired woman opened the door.

'Is Annie in?' he asked.

'Annie? My Annie? Aye.' She called through to the bedroom, 'Annie, there's a wee boy here to see you!'

She came. She was wearing a blue dressing-gown and was brushing her hair with a brush that had a mother-of-pearl back on it. Seeing her brought on a small panic and he was afraid his mouth would dry up and he would be unable to speak.

'Oh, hello,' she said, leaning forward, peering into the gloom of the landing and frowning as she tried to place him. Then she smiled and her glorious white teeth were shining. 'I know you, don't I? You're from up 30.'

She sounded posh, and he was afraid he would betray

himself in all his awful commonness when he spoke. He could feel the sweat prickling on his thighs, his stomach, his chest.

'Aye, I was in the front row last night. I brought you some comics for a len.'

'Comics?'

'Cowies. Six *Monty Hales* and six *Rocky Lanes*. Maybe you've read them before.'

'No, no but I like comics.'

She put her brush down on the hallstand and reached out for them. Out of her garish cowgirl makeup she was even more beautiful – fresh and freckled and somehow more cowgirlish than ever.

'Monty Hale's my real favourite,' he said as he handed them over. 'His horse is called Cyclone. But I like Rocky Lane as well. He's got a horse called Pardner, but his hat's a bit stupit-looking.'

'Thanks very much. I like reading comics in my bed at night, they help me to get to sleep.'

'You can have them for a week. I'll come back for them next Saturday.'

He turned to go, desperate now to get away, but she stopped him.

'Just a minute. Come here.'

Her teeth were wonderful in the semi-dark, and he felt himself dying.

'Come in a minute,' she said. 'I don't bite.'

She took him into her bedroom, sat on the bed and motioned him to sit beside her. The room was small – a single bed with a locker, a wardrobe, a small chair. Behind the headboard of the bed were photographs of her in her various cowgirl-outfits.

'I have to go some messages for my mammy,' he said.

'OK. Would you like a picture?'

He nodded.

'What's your name?'

'John.'

'John what?'

'Findlay.'

'Right, John Findlay. If I give you my nicest picture will you promise to keep it for ever, right next to your bed?'

'Aye,' he said, and meant it.

She reached above the headboard and took down a picture – herself in full regalia, with a six-gun in each hand.

'Ta,' he said, grabbing for it.

'Hold your hurry,' she said. 'I've got to sign it.' She took a pen from the locker-drawer and wrote across the pale background on the left side of the photograph: 'To John, with love and kisses, from Annie MacGinty.' She made six crosses under her signature, then handed him the photograph.

He could not bear to look at her now, he had to go.

'Will you be in next Saturday?' he asked.

'Yes, but come a bit later, OK? I usually have a wee long lie on Saturdays.'

'Right. Cheerio.'

'Cheerio, and thanks for the comics.'

And having nothing to do for his mother, he walked the four blocks home in a tearful daze of singing delight and complicated guilt.

When she answered his knock at eleven the following Saturday she was wearing a white blouse and a short black skirt and was made up, not with the coarse cowgirl-paint, but with a hint of lipstick and a touch of colour that did nothing to hide her freckles. He sat on her bed again and she tossed her long thick pony-tail across her shoulder and asked if he liked it.

'I like it best when your hair tumbles doon your back and roon your shoulders,' he said.

'Oh?' she said, affecting hurt and reaching back to undo her ribbon. 'If that's the way you feel – and here was me thinking I was doing something special, just for you.'

'Naw, leave it,' he said, panicking, 'I like it like that as well. I like pony-tails, I like your hair, and your face, and . . . everything.' His cheeks were burning, and he bent his head to his chest.

'John,' she said. 'John.' She put her finger under his chin, trying to ease his head up, but he resisted. 'My, you're a real wee snowdrop aren't you? That's what I'm going to call you, Wee Snowdrop. Come on, look at me . . . please.'

He looked up into her green eyes. They were not laughing.

'Are you a wee wee bit in love with me, Snowdrop?'

He tried to lower his head again, but she kept her finger under his chin, and she was strong. 'It's all right. I don't mind. I like it, really I do, I'm really pleased. What age are you?'

'Nine.'

'Nine? Oh my goodness, I'm nearly nineteen. I'm an old granny compared with you.'

'You are not. My sister's eighteen. She's been eighteen for ages.'

'All right well, I'm not a granny. I'm just an old big sister.' She picked up a comic. 'I like Monty Hale best as well. He looks like you, he's got a nice wee face.'

'I've got loads merr. I'll bring them next week.'

'That'll be lovely. Listen, you can come a bit earlier next week – my mother'll be away at her sister's for the weekend.'

'OK.' He stood up from the bed. 'I've got to get some messages for my mammy,' he lied again. He gathered up his comics. At the door he stopped and found the courage for his question: 'Are you just a cowgirl?'

She laughed.

'A full-time professional, you mean? No, I work at a hairdresser's in the town. Most of the other girls have to work Saturdays, but they let me off because of my career – they think I attract customers, being so famous.' She arched her eyebrows, mocking herself.

'I know,' he said.

'I'd like to become a full-time cowgirl someday. Maybe in Canada – they've got big rodeos there.'

She took him by the arm, stopping him from opening the door.

'Would you like a kiss?'

'Naw.'

'Sure? Just a wee tiny one? On the cheek? I won't tell anybody.'

'M-m.'

'Oh well, I'll just be in a huff all day now.'

He was desperate. 'Can I see your lasso next week?' he blurted.

'Oh, I don't know about that – I'm in a huff, you know. It's not every day I get rebuffed.'

Then, seeing his tears about to come and sparing him that humiliation, she took his head in both her hands and tugged his ears gently and said, 'Of course you can see it, you daft thing. Don't give me that petted lip.' She pushed him through the door.

At the top of the stairs he stopped and asked, 'Whit time will I come?'

'When do you do your mammy's messages?'

'Early,' he said, blushing.

'Well come early.'

The weather was fine in the evening and they played

Willie Woodbine. He hated the cigarette connection, but liked the game because he could react faster and hop more strongly than any of the others. Still tightly tuned from the morning, he hopped like a demon and found himself the last survivor, Craven A, having to hop across the street alone, through a forest of hostile matches. He felt Joan Reid watching him from behind, from her window-sill, and when his name was called he shot from the pavement fast, not directly across into the massed matches but at a sharp angle to the right, uphill, to take advantage of his speed. It was a good ploy: the matches on that side were mostly girls and smaller boys, too light or too timid to unbalance him, and they impeded the heavier brigade when it tried to hop uphill to head him off. He brushed aside two light-weight challenges, then survived a moderately serious assault from Dom Ruskin. Peter Simpson and Sniffer O'Hara, old hands, had headed for the far side, to cover his landing-point. Sniffer was lumbering and slow, but big and not easy to round, while Pete was almost as nimble as himself. His legs were aching from the rapid uphill hop, and he knew that he did not have much distance left and that his only hope was the direct route straight between them. He gathered himself for the final spurt, feinted to the right to unbalance Sniffer, then got between them in a single long hop.

He was two feet from the pavement and already exulting when Pete's foot caught him on the shin. Half-expecting the treachery, he was able to take most of the fall on his hands. He did not feel particularly angry, but felt he had to go through the ritual motions.

'You cheating bastit, Peter Simpson, I'll kill you for that.'

'Whit? It was an accident.'

'Accident my fucking arse, you're always doing it, you cannae take a beating, you bastit.'

Pete was all hurt innocence and he turned to Sniffer. 'Michael, tell him it was an accident. Honest to God, John, I never meant it.'

Sniffer, who liked fights, shrugged non-committally. But John's indignation was already dying, he was in the mood neither for fight nor huff. 'Right, I'll let you aff this time, you bastit, but I'm no playing with cheaters – I'm having a rest.'

He crossed the street to where Joan sat on her sill. Seeing his intention, she moved to make a space for him beside her.

'That was terrible, John,' she said, leaning across to look at his hand. 'Is it awful sore?'

'Na,' he said, becoming Randolph Scott as he spoke, 'just a scratch.'

'But you better clean it in case it festers. Here's my hanky.'

'It's OK Joan, honest, you don't want a lot of blood on your hanky.'

'It's already full of blood. I had a nose bleed this morning, a really bad one.'

So he let her dab his graze with her blood-stained handkerchief and felt her happiness and wondered how he could start the conversation he knew they must have soon.

'There,' she said, after a happy silent minute, 'that's the bleeding stopped.'

He decided on the sudden plunge.

'Would you like to go to Canada, Joan?'

She puckered her brow, solemnly considering the question.

'Naw, I don't think so.'

'How no? It's great there.'

'But I like it here. My Aunty Alice knows a woman that went tae Canada and she hated it and she came straight back.'

'She was a bampot. It's great out there – no like this.'

She smiled her soft smile and he read it and it said: I like this, but. I like this, and I like sitting here with you on my warm window-sill and you a wounded soldier and me with my hanky. This is what I like, but I know you're different, so it's OK, you can tell me.

'Well listen.' He almost, but did not, reach forward to put his hand on her knee. 'I thought I might just sort of, go there, when I'm big, like, for a while.'

'That's OK.'

'Just for a while. I'll likely come back.'

She smiled with her thin lips and her gently squint eyes (Annie MacGinty had round green eyes and glorious white teeth and bright red lips) and, braver than he, she placed her good left hand on his knee.

Released, he felt no immediate joy, but figured he could cope with the guilt.

He rapped the knocker timidly at quarter-past nine the following Saturday morning and heard a little yelp of mock-panic from inside the house.

'Just a minute,' she called, 'I'm not ready yet.'

Then the door opened and she stood framed in the doorway in full magnificent regalia.

'I thought if you were to see my lasso you might as well see the lot. Come in and tell me what you think. What time is it?'

'You said to come early,' he said, stepping into the hall.

'Yes, yes, but don't you know a girl needs her beauty sleep on a Saturday morning?'

They were in her bedroom. The door of the wardrobe was open and there was a full-length mirror inside. She checked her appearance briefly, then twirled for him.

'What do you think, then?'

It was a costume he had not seen before: white stetson,

white blouse, bright yellow waistcoat with green fringes, green kerchief, yellow sequinned skirt, yellow boots studded with emeralds.

'You must've been nearly ready when I came,' he said. 'You were only a minute.'

'You're a fly wee thing, aren't you? So I was – I only had my lipstick to do.' She dabbed her lips a few times, finishing her makeup. 'So come on then – when a girl goes to such a lot of trouble she expects a few compliments from her boyfriend. What do you think?'

'It's great.'

'Great, eh? Oh well, I suppose that'll have to do. Sit down and tell me what you've been up to.'

They sat on the bed and he told her about school, about his family, about his friends, his wild-animal books, his comics. On the brink of telling her about Joan he stopped.

'Can I see your lasso now?'

'Right you are – anything to oblige a gentleman.'

She brought it from the wardrobe and her hands were sure and clever even in the lifting of it.

'It's really white, i'n't it?' he said.

'Yes, and it feels different from an ordinary rope. See?'

He took it from her.

'It's sort of stiff and loose at the same time,' he said.

'That's right. It's got to be really supple. There's hardly any room in here, but we can try a wee low-spin. You watch.'

She took the rope from him and laid a circular noose, a yard across, on the carpet, holding the rest in her right hand.

'It's quite hard to explain, really, but it's easy to do. You just give your wrist a wee flick and it comes up. See.'

Still perfectly circular, the noose was spinning magically a few inches above the floor. 'Then when you're quite sure about that you can try a few tricks.'

She stepped inside the noose and it was twirling around her ankles.

'Now you come in. Step nice and high and stand really close to me.'

Trembling, he stepped across the noose and moved in until their bodies were almost touching. 'A bit closer,' she said. 'It's only a wee loop.'

He moved in until they were touching, with his chin and nose resting in the hollow between her breasts. He was afraid to breathe.

'Whee!' she said, and the loop began to move up and down, from the floor to the level of his shoulders, and he could feel her breast moving against his left cheek as she raised and lowered her arm. Then she stopped and they were standing together in the perfect circle of the noose.

'Now you have a shot,' she said, stepping back and handing him the end of the rope. He held it as he had seen her do and flicked his wrist as she had done hers and the rope flopped uselessly and the circle was ruined. He tried twice more, with the same effect, then she stood behind him.

'Wait and I'll help you a bit,' she said. She took his hands in hers. 'You hold this one out here for balance, and you hold the rope quite loose in this one, then you just . . . flick.'

The rope came up and with her hand doing the work, began to spin.

'There now. I'll take my hand away and you've got to keep it twirling. Right?'

He could not talk.

'OK?'

'OK.'

She stepped back. The rope spun for a few frenetic seconds, then flopped. She clapped her hands. 'Not bad for a learner,' she said. 'One more try.'

She held him again, and this time stayed with him longer, while he found the rhythm. That rhythm passed through them: he could feel her breasts warm against the back of his head, her strong clever arms against the full length of his, her thighs against his buttocks. And as the rope spun and he felt control of it pass gradually from her hands to his, he told her with his arms, his shoulders, his head: I'm coming to Canada with you and you can be a cowgirl in the rodeos and I'll be at the school – then when I'm big I'll marry you and I'll be a doctor or a filmstar or something and we'll live on a big ranch and then I'll kiss you.

And he was twirling it by himself, effortlessly, till he saw her in front of him, laughing and applauding, and he looked up and lost the rhythm and the rope flopped against his legs.

'Lovely,' she said. 'You'll make a smashing wee cowboy, you're a really quick learner.'

He let the end of the rope drop.

'When are you gaun tae Canada?' he asked.

'Canada? Oh, that depends on my boyfriend.'

The word hit him like a stone in the stomach. 'Have you got a boyfriend?'

'Oh yes, a smashing one. He's called Robert and he's over six-foot.'

'I've never seen him at the concerts.'

'No. He goes out to the pub with his friends every Friday. Saturday's winching day for us. We go to the shops in the afternoon, then we go dancing at night, or if I've got a show he comes to that, then we maybe go to a party or something afterwards.'

He was finding it hard to stem the tears, to make words.

'Is he going to Canada with you?'

'Too true he is. In fact, it's really me that's going with him, it was his idea in the first place. He's in the yards just now, in John Brown's, but he's joining the police. He's going for his tests and things next week, but he'll get in no bother, being so big and strong.'

'My brother tried for the polis, but he failed his eyesight.'

'What a shame. My Bobby – I've started calling him that for a laugh now – Bobby the bobby – he's got really good eyesight, he can see see for miles, he's got a car and everything. Anyway, he thought he could join the police here then we could get engaged and then in a year we could emigrate to Canada and he could be a Mounty and I could be a rodeo girl.'

'Aye.' He reached up frantically to catch a tear, and she saw, and took his hand.

'Hey, what's this we're getting? What's wrong with you?'

'Nothing.'

'Don't you nothing me, my Wee Snowdrop – I know something when I see it. You're upset about me having another boyfriend, aren't you?'

He forced his chin down, hard against his chest.

'Come on, Snowdrop, look at me – look up.'

He would not.

'If you don't look up I'll start crying as well – then where will we be?'

Her eyes were big with mascara, and magnified through his tears. She touched his nose with her finger.

'Listen, you daft thing, you're my *other* boyfriend. I love you as well.'

'But you're going to Canada with him – with that Robert.'

'But he's the same age as me, see? Some day you'll be a big six-footer and you'll have a girlfriend your own age and you'll forget about me.'

'I'm the wee-est boy in my class.'

'That doesn't matter. Robert was the wee-est in his class. Just you eat your porridge and lots of butter and you'll soon be the biggest.'

'I hate butter. It scunners me.'

'Oh. Well, you'll have to learn to like it. You need butter to make you grow big and strong. My daddy always used to say it lubricates your whole system, like oil in a machine.'

'I hate margarine even worse.'

He let the tears flow now, and she put her arms around him and cradled him to her breast and rocked him.

'There, there,' she said, and her voice was gravel-lovely, 'don't be daft, Robert's a lovely boy, you'd like him a lot, you really would. And you want me to be happy, don't you?'

He nodded against her blouse.

'Well then, you can be my other boyfriend – my *wee* boyfriend. Are you coming to the concert next Friday?'

He nodded again.

'Right. You get a seat right in the front and I'll sing every song specially for you and give you a special wink. OK?'

Again he nodded, and she hugged him tighter, and there was a knock on the door.

'Oh help,' she said, letting him go. 'That'll be Bobby – what time is it?' He didn't know, and she went to the door.

Bobby was big and frowning, in a dark suit and polished shoes.

'You're early,' she said, tilting her head for a kiss.

'What the hell you up to?' he said, noticing her cowgirl gear, ignoring her gesture.

'Oh this? I was just having some fun with my wee pal. Remember I told you about him – wee John?'

'Oh aye.' He stepped towards the bed, a huge and lowering shape in the small room, and looked down at the small boy who was desperately drying the tear-stains from his cheeks.

'Well fuck off, wee John,' he said quietly.

'Robert! Don't talk to the boy like that, that's terrible,' she said.

'Oh terrible is it? Well how about this?' He bent down, close to the boy's face, and made his voice even softer, and used a mock-polite accent:

'Wee John, you've had your fun. Now would you mind getting off that bed, and out that door, before I break your fucking wee neck and throw you out the window?'

She brushed past him and took the stunned and frightened boy by the hand and ushered him to the door. Through his own tears he could see hers.

'You better go, he's not always like this, honest he's not. I'll see you at the concert.'

Suddenly he was in the landing, and cold, and the door was closed and through it he heard her voice, muffled but loud with anger and tearful, saying, 'You're a rotten swine, so you are!' Then the inner door slammed and shut him off from their argument.

He was at the door of Pensioners' Hall half-an-hour before McGlashen opened it on the Friday evening, and he ran to the centre seat of the front row. He became caught up despite himself in the kiltie songs and the Pat Mick and the Irishman jokes and the impersonations of Dickie Valentine's impersonations and when she appeared and the Hall exploded he was hot and happy and she winked at him and he wondered if she noticed he'd grown bigger and stronger by force-feeding himself with bread and butter all week.

Then it was the final encore and she was twirling the rope over her head and they were singing themselves hoarse:

Let him go, let him tarry
Let him sink or let him swim.
He doesn't care for me
Nor I don't care for him.
He can go and find another
That I hope he will enjoy
For I'm going to marry
A far nicer boy!

In the end, as had become tradition, they were silent while she stood with her arms raised and her legs apart in her strong cowgirl stance and boomed in her wonderful gravelly voice:

I'm going to marry
A far nicer boy!

And as the curtain closed on her for the last time she looked at him, hot and happy in the front row, and winked.

The Sweary-man's Gold

Somebody up there either didn't like Sniffer O'Hara or had plans for him that embraced more than a mere seventy-year sojourn among the cat's pee. He had a good half-dozen near escapes before he finally died seven days before his sixteenth birthday, in search of the Sweary-man's gold.

The Sweary-man spent the summer months under the bridge that spanned the canal behind Alexandra Parade. During these months the path under the bridge was virtually closed to walkers because he was ferociously jealous about his patch and would shower intruders with the vilest imprecations and the most horrific threats.

Adults could see the desperate frailness of the old man under his tent of a raincoat and his three-foot beard and laugh at the threats, but for the children he was a genuine terror, a fire-breathing monster. And the legend was spawned that he was, indeed, a metamorphosed dragon, protecting a fabulous treasure that was stowed in the stonework of the bridge. Sniffer died because he was old enough in body to see through the threats, and young enough in mind to believe the legend. Younger, slyer children fed him morsels of the story, told tales of how they had come across the Sweary-man counting his gold, and he, with a token-show of disbelief, swallowed them. He sensed rightly that he was chosen to carry out the quest alone, a squireless Knight, because he alone had courage enough and faith enough.

On a dusky June evening he took a breadknife from the

sideboard drawer while Elsie, his mother, was busy peeling potatoes at the sink, slung two gas-mask satchels from the wardrobe over his shoulder, and went up the stairs to the Findlay's to borrow Alastair's bike, which had a big saddlebag for transporting the gold and a five-speed gear for a quick getaway.

He was pulling away from the kerb outside the close when Elsie, still at the sink, noticed him and opened the window and called down to him. There was no reprimand, no message: it was an automatic reaction for mothers to open the windows, to shout down, to make mother-noises.

'Is that you, Michael? You aw right, son?'

Sniffer stopped the bike four feet into the Road, looked up at the window and cupped his hands around his mouth to call back.

At the moment when he had been stealing the knife from the sideboard drawer, young Gerry McCann had been stealing the keys for the new coal-lorry from the rack in his father's garage in Glenfield Street. His plan was not particularly outrageous – a quick spin up to Springburn, a toot of the horn to bring down Marylin, his latest, a run as far as Bishopbriggs, a stop in a country lane for some not-too-heavy winching (it being midweek), then back to the garage before his old man left the pub. He did stop at the junction, did glance fleetingly leftwards before swinging the lorry into the Road, but it was a gloomy night and Alastair Findlay's bike had no lights and Sniffer was facing the wrong way.

Elsie screamed and covered her eyes and was blessedly spared the sight of her youngest being killed. The impact as young McCann accelerated away from the corner was not especially violent, but Sniffer and the bike rose in the air all entangled with each other, and some part of the frame caught him in the throat and sliced his windpipe. At the same time his chin thrust hard against the handle of the breadknife that he had hidden inside his jumper and the blade buried itself in his abdomen.

Gerry did not stop the lorry, but continued to accelerate towards the traffic lights, passed through them on red, and headed for Springburn and Marylin's comforting breasts. Sniffer died in the Royal Infirmary while they were trying to sew him together.

Alastair had to get up a half-hour earlier for the next six weeks and walk to work until he had saved enough to get a new front wheel for his bike.

The Sweary-man cursed and threatened a long summer through and on the last day of September went away for the winter.

THE END

ITS COLOURS THEY ARE FINE
by Alan Spence

First published to wide critical acclaim in 1977, *Its Colours They Are Fine* has since become a classic of Glaswegian fiction. Its three interlinked stories cover every aspect of life in the city, vividly evokling the slums and its inhabitants, both young and old, Catholic and Protestant, the hopeful and the disillusioned. The first section of the book has been hailed as 'the definitive recreation of a Glasgow childhood'. It describes a violent upbringing in the slums which translates in early adulthood to brawls at dance halls, the bustle and pomp of an Orange march, a Catholic Wedding and finally to the quiet and tranquillity amongst the exotic plants and statues in the Kibble Palace.

Alan Spence's writing throughout is powerful and moving, full of poetry, and with an imaginative life which transforms the book's bleak urban setting into something warm, tender and humorous.

0 552 13012 5

THE CHIC MURRAY STORY
THE BEST WAY TO WALK
by Andrew Yule

'Half hilarious, half sad . . . an accurate likeness of an extraordinary talent'
Scottish Field

For more than forty years Chic Murray made people laugh. Not just in Scotland but wherever he went. Whether you knew him in the early days when he and his wife Maidie toured the halls as the comedy duo 'The Tall Droll and the Small Doll', or whether you encountered him more recently in *Gregory's Girl* or one of the many films and stage parts that came his way late in his career, you are unlikely to forget his unique brand of madness.

Andrew Yule's bestselling biography charts Chic Murray's rise from his humble beginnings in Greenock to become a legend in his own lifetime. Since his tragic death in 1985, the cult has intensified and been passed on to a whole new generation. *The Best Way to Walk*, at once a tender love story and an uproarious celebration of a truly original comic genius, will show you exactly why fellow comedians and adoring fans alike echo Billy Connolly's view that Chic is still 'the master'.

'For the many Murrayphiles, the book is an invaluable thesaurus of the man, his lives and his work'
Rikki Fulton – *Scotsman*

0 552 13720 0